Being Delilah by Maya Avery is something serious. Charlie is self-serving, straight forward, mysterious, direct, compassionate, loving, and protective. She is what I call a multi-dimensional character. She gives it to you raw, whether you like it or not. It's the evolution of Charlie and her relationships that makes this book a page turner.

—Robyn Day

"I had compassion for Charlie immediately. Terrance, Ian, and George deserved exactly what they received."

—A. Jenkins

"I was stuck and shook. The ending will have you pissed, scared, happy, and feeling the heart of Charlie."

—Ajah Imon

"*Being Delilah* is a whirlwind of emotions. She got what she wanted by any means necessary."

—Nikki Penn

"I was drawn in until the end. I couldn't stop reading."

—M. Lawton, Jr.

"It's a must-read. I'm ready for the sequel. This gives me Sistah Souljah vibes."

—Ursula Lawton

"As a man, I wasn't expecting to pull in like this. I went from pissed to rooting for Charlie."

—Kenyon Fairley

"This is a non-stop page turner. Charlie gave 'em hell and then some."

—Alexandria Jackson

"I didn't know whether to feel sorry for Charlie or the men she fawked over. I love a woman who uses what she's got to get what she wants. I was drawn in instantly."

—S. Applewhite

BEING

Delilah

Naomi,

Thank you for your support and love!
you are abundantly blessed and favored
to get your blessing sis!

769-572-2084

BEING

Delilah

MAYA AVERY

Bowie, MD

Paperback ISBN: 978-0-578-81374-5

Published by Maya Avery
Bowie, MD

Printed in the United States of America
First Edition March 2021

Cover Design by: Make Your Mark Publishing Solutions
Interior Layout by: Make Your Mark Publishing Solutions

ACKNOWLEDGEMENTS

would like to acknowledge and praise, first, God for giving me the creativity and girth to write out my pain. My children for standing behind me, in front of me, and on the side of me, pushing me to the finish line. To my mom, Ursula Lawton, who allowed me to put this in writing and added her 50 cents and stamp of approval. To my brothers and sisters, who said from day one, "Write your heart out, sister; we stand for you." Shout out to Alexandria, Oky Iwundu, Dejuan, Paulette, Nichole, and Nia for keeping me grounded and sane during this process. To Sterling Photography for the bomb image used for the book cover and for being completely okay with me expressing my vision. He nailed it. And to a plethora of friends and family who cheered me on.

I dedicate this book to my granny, Clemis Avery. You first taught me how to love and forgive. I remembered, Grandmother. Thank you for being my guardian angel.

TRIGGER WARNING

The following content includes scenes of rape, molestation, and explicit language.

PREFACE

Being a whore isn't easy,
but so many of us do it!

he Hot Spot: I grew up thinking the tiny space I occupied in Wiggins, Mississippi (the Bible Belt area) was truly all the world had to offer. Although my parents weren't absent from my life, I was primarily raised by my grandmother. Regrettably, love didn't help me academically, mentally, or emotionally. I was lost, stuck, and misunderstood. Floating through life battling dyslexia, low self-esteem, and spiritual battles. Can you imagine living in a small town that celebrated the KKK weekly, had a rated-D educational system, and where most young girls like me relived scenes from the movie, *The Color Purple*? This was a norm in the early eighties. However, I was completely happy being raised by my grandmother, with no care in the world. Her warm embrace, sweet kisses, and ohhh, not to forget the prayers! The prayers and hymns were such sweet melodies to my ears. I can hear her voice now, whispering prayers in my ear. I miss her. Her prayers are what brought me through hard times. Grandma's prayers are what kept me after the rape, molestation, adultery, hoeing, mental illness, including my anger issues, and the rebuilding of who I am and whose I am.

The stages of Charlie's life will give you insight on how to overcome the fabrication of who you are and become your authentic self. Yeah, I know you may not consider yourself to be a whore, hoe, thot, or any of the above mentioned. However, you have this book because your inner voice told you that you needed to read it. Let's go on this journey of discovering our true selves. Grab your tea or preferred beverage and a blankie. Put your *Do Not Disturb* sign on the door and enjoy the turbulence. I promise you that the landing will be smooth.

CHAPTER 1

Manipulation is a tactic I learned at an early age. I was born Charlie MacClemore. My grandmother gave me the nickname "Mighty." She said "mighty" meant to possess great strength and power. Lord knows she was right; I needed all the strength I could get. At eight years old, I was introduced to sex. No actual penetration but exposure to male body parts and humping. One day after school, my granny had gone into town with one of my aunts to purchase groceries. My granny could not drive, so she depended on her family to take her to and from. My fourteen-year-old cousin Franko was my caregiver when my granny was gone into town. This particular day, an uncomfortable feeling of fear came over me. I literally couldn't shake this feeling. I believe the events of this day were a preamble to my introduction to low self-esteem and being fearful in all ways. I arrived home, scouting through the house to see if Franko was there. After not seeing him, a sigh of relief came over me. I really loved him; he was family. I would do anything for him. I denote, I was only eight. In my mind, we were the only people who existed in the world, us, and anyone within a forty-five-mile radius. The feeling of relief was short-lived, because not even five minutes later, he walked through the door. I took a big gulp of water, said, "Hey" and ran out the back door. I needed to talk to Jesus, as I did daily.

"Jesus, I will name all of my dolls Mary, but not my children, if you just protect me. Amen." Looking back, the prayer was quite silly, but he did what I asked. The hedge of protection guarded me all the days of my life.

Suddenly, I heard Franko call out my name. "Mighty, where are you at? Where is you going, gul?"

"I wanna play outside with my JoJo and Mahalia. Dey on the way up the hill in a minute," I lied, as I needed to concoct a story that I thought would be free from his games. To my dismay, however, he outwitted me with his response.

"JoJo and Mahalia just called. I told dem Granny not home yet … to come later. So, come inside for a minute."

Pebbles of sweat formed across my forehead, and I could feel my heart race. Slowly and dreadfully, I walked inside.

"Do you want to do it?"

Fear engulfed me. I couldn't utter a response.

"You know, do it … hump … play mamma and daddy?"

He usually would dry hump me and make me say,

"Uh uhuh uhu uh," until he stopped humping me. But this time, he added a special "touch."

"Pull your pants down. I wanna show you something I saw on television," he said as he unbuckled his belt and unbuttoned and dropped his ole nasty Wrangler jeans.

I was still gripped with fear … to the point that I couldn't respond.

Taking my silence for a no, he made an offer. "If you do it, I'll let you go outside … buy you an ice cream and take you to Cousin JoJo and Mahalia's house.

"And if I don't?" I challenged.

"I'm gonna make you do it anyway.

Grudgeful, I retreated.

He chuckled at the THURSDAY panties I had on. "Girl, you too grown to wear draws with the days of the week on dem."

That didn't stop what happened next.

He climbed on top of me, humping real fast, making me make the "uhh, uhh, uhh" noise.

"What if I get pregnant?" I whispered in between uh, huh, um, uhh sounds.

"Gul, you ain't gone get no pregnant. You not bleeding monthly yet."

I lay there making the noises he'd instructed me to make, while at the same time, wondering about what he meant by bleeding monthly. After a while, he stopped and gave me the usual "after molestation" speech.

"Remember, don't you tell nobody."

I nodded. The tears began to roll, and I began to cry hard and loud.

"Mighty, I'm sorry. I'm sorry. I didn't mean to make you cry. You know that, gul, don't ya? Hey, look. I'll never do it again. You know I'd never hurtcha," he said, as he wiped my tears. His fingers smelled like bleach. At the time, I figured it was probably from the white stuff that I saw coming out of his private part.

A sigh of relief swept my face when I heard the car door close. It was my granny and aunt returning from town with groceries. Boy, was I ever so excited to hear that car door slam and my granny call out my name. She'd say my name as if she was singing a hymn by the Temptations ... "My girl, Mighhhty, my girl, where are you?"

Once again, Franko begged me to not tell Granny. "Please, Mighty, please don't tell. I just wanted to know about it. The boys at school were talking about it. I just wanted to try it."

And just like that, I was introduced to manipulation ... how it makes you feel guilty about turning in your abuser or the one who violates you. How the perpetrator uses it to make you feel sorry for them. Now all you have to do is make up a good story and become the victim.

This was Lesson One. I would learn to do the same. In my life, I learned that all I had to do was give a guy a good story, be demanding, and fake repentance to get what I wanted. Ohhh this was going to be too easy.

CHAPTER 2

ast forward to adulthood. I recall this one particular guy. Let's call him Ralph. Ralph had the hots for me, baby! He wrote me love notes and would leave them on my car. I mean, in the 80s and 90s, the only way to convey our feelings was through pen and paper and music. He gave me money, took me out on dates. After every date, he asked me to come in for a minute. I politely declined every time. I knew he wanted to have sex, but I held him off. That is, until I really needed my rent and light bill paid. I had plans for my money and didn't want to spend my own money to pay my bills. My friends and I planned this big trip to D.C. I needed every dime. This was when I decided to use that skill of manipulation on Ralph. I knew Ralph had the money … he bragged about it often.

I always said that my nose wasn't big for no reason. I could sniff a man out with low self-esteem, plenty of money, and who needed a PYT (pretty young thing) on his arm to parade around. I was that PYT every man needed.

I would make any man feel like God placed him in the center of the earth and the world bowed to his feet.

I met Ralph when I attended a social event with a guy I was dating. In my mind, Brad wasn't my ideal man. As a matter of fact, he was a bum in my book, but he had a sexy body and sex with him was everything! While at this event, Ralph accidentally knocked my beverage out of my hand and onto my new dress. I was livid … pissed to the highest piss-tiv-vity. I scowled at Ralph to get napkins to clean the mess up and demanded money for my dress. Without thinking, Ralph pulled out three hundred dollars and handed it to me. He undoubtedly thought I was wearing a designer dress. But truth be told, I bought it from Arden B, and it was on sale for fifty dollars. I pretended to be so upset, even after receiving the money. I was using the trick of manipulation to the hills.

Ralph was no looker by any means. He was tall, skinny—boney skinny—had caramel skin, bad teeth, and bad taste in clothing. However, after his apology, he and I exchanged dialogue. He turned out to be smart and well established. He graduated from Hampton U. Had a great job, no children, no girlfriend, and no family in the area. Perfect! Bingo! Got him! After pretending to calm down, I gave Ralph a long, hard stare. He looked innocent. My man radar kicked in. I could tell he was a "softy." He looked at me like I was the most beautiful girl in the world.

"Are you here alone?" he asked, looking deep into my eyes, almost as if he was looking through me.

"Why?" I asked in a snooty tone.

"Well, I was thinking I could take you home to change your clothes, since I spilled a drink on you."

"No, thank you. However, I appreciate your thoughtfulness," I said, winking and strutting off. I knew that complimenting his chivalry and gentleness and stroking his ego would spark more interest and cause him to chase. Like clockwork, he ran behind me.

"Hey ... hey... it was nice talking to you. What's your name?"

I turned around, acting as though I was surprised.

"Can I have your number?"

"For what?" I said, making him gravel, so to speak.

"I wanna call you ... take you out on a date," he said nervously.

"I'mma give you my number, but I won't be available for a few weeks. Just keep calling until I answer," I said, digging in my purse for a pen and paper.

Ralph did just that. He called several times ... until I finally answered. I knew I had him. I put my plan in motion right away. We went on several dates, and I knew Ralph was dying to see the inside of my place and smell the inside of my place. I devised a plan to let him but not for what he thought. I purposely did not let Ralph get too close. There were no passionate kisses or sexual intercourse between us for several months. I limited the physical activity to hugs and cheek kisses, nothing more. So, I had him right where I wanted him.

When Ralph asked me out to lunch one day, I decided that I would ask him for the money for my trip that day. During our lunch date, I mentioned the trip and the associated cost to Ralph.

"Sounds like fun," Ralph said. He didn't make any mention about the cost. Money wasn't an issue for him.

"Yeah, I hope so … been planning this for a while."

Ralph kept eating. "Who's going?" Ralph asked. I supposed he wanted to make sure he wasn't giving me money to go on a trip with some other guy. No problem. So, I told him.

"Me and my girls. Well, I hope I can make it," I managed to slip in. You see, I had to set him up to ask the obvious—why I was uncertain about being able to go on the trip.

"Well, what would keep you from going? Why do you have to hope?" he asked.

Bingo. He fell right into the trap. "Money," I said in a somber tone. "My money is acting funny," I added.

Ralph was silent. Maybe he wasn't as naïve as I thought. I sat silent as I fidgeted with my fingers. Then, I decided to be bold. I mean, by this time, Ralph had bought new tires for my car, financed several shopping trips, paid tuition for my daughter, all on a voluntary basis. It was quite natural for me to assume that he had me this time. I mean, why not? Finally, I went for the gusto. "Ralph, can you give me thirteen hundred for my trip?"

He had to have been waiting for me to ask. He quickly responded, "Yes … if you let me cum inside you. I wanna be with you. You barely look at me in the face, Mighty. I wanna feel you."

My stomach turned flips of disgust. Did he just say "cum inside of me?" Did he just question why I don't look at him in the face? I was offended and insulted. I think I may have even been pissed. I know I was wrong, but my goodness gracious. I literally had to purposely schedule dates with Ralph during times when the sun was brightest, so I could wear shades, just so I didn't have to look at him eye to eye.

I counted to ten in my head. I was trying my hardest not to lose my cool. After all, I needed that money from Ralph. After I cooled down on the inside, I responded. I made a counteroffer. "Ralph, I'll let you come inside me under one condition."

Ralph's eyes lit up. He seemed as though he could almost grab the words out of my mouth before I could utter them. "What?" he said, drawing closer to me.

"You gotta give me the cash first. To be completely honest with you, I have a fuck partner and an emergency dick in a jar that I use at my leisure. If you wanna replace either of them, you gotta come with it." I just came out with it. We were going to play by my rules and my rules only.

To my surprise, there was no further discussion about my request-slash-proposition. Ralph jumped at the opportunity. He requested the check, paid the bill, and dropped me back off at work. Before driving off, he said, "I'll be at your place when you get home with the money, plus extra."

He was willing to reach deep in his pockets just to be able to come inside my place. But what he didn't know was that it was going to take more than money, lunch, and shopping for me to give up my precious jewels to him. In my mind, I wasn't going to spread my legs just because a man was doing what he was supposed to do. That is, take care of his woman … or in my case, for the woman he wanted.

Just as he promised, Ralph was at my door waiting for me when I got off work. He had flowers, a card, and a bag of clothes. I assumed that he had the money, too, but it was in his wallet. I knew that if he kept it up, he was gonna make future refusals, on my part, difficult. That was, if I could get past his bad taste in clothes, cologne, and his annoying energy.

"Where is the money, honey?" I said, grabbing the flowers and card and tossing them on the kitchen table as we entered the house.

With a big Kool Aid smile, Ralph reached in his pocket, retrieved his wallet, pulled out a wad of cash, and handed it to me.

"Is this thirteen hundred?" I asked, swinging the wad of cash back and forth.

"No … it's thirteen hundred plus an extra two hundred. So altogether, it's fifteen hundred," Ralph said with a smile.

I almost did a somersault right in the kitchen.

I told him, "I'll be right back." I ran upstairs and hid the money in my daughter's room. Then I ran back downstairs to tell another lie. "Ralph, my daughter will be home at eight thirty. We're gonna have to do this another night," I said in a pretend somber tone. Truth be told, it was my ex's night to keep her, so my daughter was not going to be nowhere near home that night. I just hoped Ralph would go for it.

"Noo, nooo, noo," Ralph said, loudly. "Tonight, Mighty! I haven't had sex in two years."

"Well, Ralph, you're not about to tonight, either. You can give me some head and jack off, but that's it," I said matter-of-factly.

Ralph sighed but complied. "Can I rub your breasts too?"

"Sure, Ralph, you got ten minutes. Then, we can talk for fifteen minutes. After that, you gotta go home."

Watching Ralph's eyes dance as I undressed gave me a sense of calmness. The touch of his hands gently stroking my breasts. His slow, deep breaths massaging my neck, leading to passionate kisses. It was as if we were making love without making actual love.

That was the best head I had ever eva, eva, eva, eva, eva … did I say eva had? Ralph's oral game was on point … to the point that he had tears rolling down my face. I almost reconsidered being with him, or at least giving in to intercourse, but not before the bag was secured—money, diamonds, pearls, bills. Yeah, I wanted it all!

With the exception of Nigel, who would screw me until he fell asleep and then wake up thirty minutes later and wanna screw again, I wasn't having sex with anyone without expecting something in return. While he didn't take me on shopping sprees, trips, or give me wads of money, he was good at doing things like fixing my car, running errands … real basic stuff.

My philosophy was simple—If you ain't paying, I am not staying. If you ain't bucking (meaning, giving up the money), then I ain't fucking.

After Ralph served that mouth game until I passed out, he recited his love for me. His words were very eloquently spoken.

"Charlie, I dreamt of having a woman like you in my life for years. I know I'm not the most attractive man, the best dressed, or have the most beautiful smile. I feel something for you I have never felt before. I think I love you, Charlie. I want to meet your daughter and your family. I know I could be all that you need in a man. I pray for you, Charlie, more than I pray for myself. You're truly my everything. I just need you to always know that I would do anything for you."

I felt bad, remorseful. But then there was a part of me that was angry. I didn't want Ralph to love me. I didn't love him. I falsely made him feel good with my hasty compliments, my fake laughs, and brilliant ego-booster tactics. Those were all lies to get what I wanted. It worked … but what about Ralph? I tried to give him his money back, but he refused. This was one of the few times I had to consider someone else, not my own self-indulging, self-righteous seeking self.

Do you wanna know what happened between Ralph and me? Well, after he told me he loved me, I changed my number and no longer accepted his letters. Instead, I had them marked "Return to Sender." I knew I was not worthy of his love. He was a good man who deserved a woman to love him back with no strings attached. I wasn't her. Ralph was too good for me. I took his money and his heart without giving anything authentic back in return. I was a thief. I purposely taunted a good man due to my own lack and childhood trauma.

About seven months had gone by when Ralph eventually stopped writing. He was on my mind a lot. I wondered how he was doing mentally and emotionally. While in the kitchen cooking breakfast one Saturday for my daughter, there was a knock at the door. My daughter rushed to the door before I could get to it first. She opened the door to find what appeared to be a stranger on the opposite side of the door.

"You're a stranger and can't come in," she politely told him.

"Who is it?" I said as I approached the door and opened it a little wider.

It was Ralph! I was in shock; I unconsciously began to smile. I felt my body getting warm from his presence. I performed a quick scan of him. He was about fifty to sixty pounds heavier, more built, and was now wearing braces. I could see his new S500 parked in front of my house.

"Hey!" I greeted, giving him a warm hug.

"Can I come in?"

"I'm sorry, but my daughter is here. I'll step out." Although I did my thing when it came to men, I shielded my daughter from what I was doing. Outside of her father, she had not seen me with a man.

"I can't?" Ralph said, shocked by my answer.

"It's not okay for you drop by unannounced."

He apologized and then shared how I'd hurt him. He shared with me the he'd lost his mother the month before we met. He said I reminded him of her. He stated he had been abused sexually as a child, how his cousin would beat him for being smart, and that he suffered from depression until he met me. His exact words were, "You brought sunshine to my darkness." He said he figured if he changed his look, I would accept him back. So, he worked out, got a personal stylist, and braces. I was gloating in my conceitedness until he continued.

"I met someone who made me feel like you made me feel."

Although I had no mirror, I was certain the smile washed right off my face. However, I tried to play the embarrassment off. "Oh, really?"

"Yep. Thanks to you. You showed me that there was someone out there for me … who would love me the same way I loved them. "Charlie, I'm trying something different … someone different."

"Well, I'm happy for you," I said. Even though he had just burst my bubble, I was happy for Ralph. So, who is she?"

Ralph turned around and motioned for the person sitting in the car to get out. The passenger door opened, and out stepped the most beautiful man I had ever laid eyes on.

I swallowed hard, trying to disguise my shock.

"Charlie, I would like you to meet Timothy. He and I are getting married in San Francisco in three months, and I would like you to be my best woman."

Needless to say, my facial expression reacted before my mouth did. "No, Ralph, I will not be your best woman."

CHAPTER 3

*D*eceitfulness is the act of being intentionally un-truthful with the intention to mislead someone.

Growing up in Mississippi wasn't as bad as folk on the East and West coast portrayed. Words in our country slang, such as "y'all, gul, howdy, and finna," are all endearing terms. Learning this lingo is sort of like a rite of passage for anyone moving down South.

I could see Jada's tall, lanky self, standing in her drive-way as we pulled up. She was so excited to see me. Her little arm was just waving so hard as she yelled out to my daddy, my little brother, Ms. Nelson, and me. My dad *had* to drive Ms. Nelson home from work. Although it seemed like my dad was doing a nice gesture, he wasn't. There was more going on between him and Ms. Nelson. They weren't fooling anybody.

"Hey, y'all," Jada shouted as our car pulled into her driveway. Her frail body leaped up and down.

We had big plans on this particular evening. I was so

eager to attend this big summer party, I jumped out the car so fast, I almost forgot my bag.

"What ya'll finna do?" Ms. Nelson asked. Jada gave a look of confusion and uncertainty, as if to say, *Why are you asking me this question, heifer*? Ms. Nelson found Jada's look to be disrespectful; she looked at my daddy with fire in her eyes.

Ms. Nelson snapped her fingers and spat out to my dad, "If you don't make Jada answer me, you know Charlie's mommy is crazy and will kill both of us for letting her leave your sight."

Ms. Nelson wasn't exaggerating. My mom sat on ten at all times, ready to come after anybody who messed with her children. My mom and her sisters had taken an all-girls trip to Mexico. I knew this would be my only opportunity to stay overnight with Jada.

My dad followed with the same question. "Who, where, and what are y'all doing tonight?"

Without hesitation, Jada replied, "We're going to a ball game."

"And where else?" my father said, not batting an eye.

"We might go to Lil Juny birthday dance."

"Oh, okay," my father replied, now looking at me. "Charlie, make sure you call me when you get in tonight. If you don't, I'm coming to get you. You hear me?!"

"Yes, sir," I replied with a smirk.

Thirteen years old at the time, all I could do was think that in five years I would be grown. Then, I wouldn't have to tell my parents anything! Besides, I knew he was just putting on a show for our audience. My dad would be in bed, knocked out by eight thirty every night, snoring and dead to the world.

As my dad and brother pulled off, I waved a good-bye so hard that my arm hurt. I really wished my daddy would've made me stay home that night.

Jada and I had been friends nearly our entire lives. Our parents were friends, having grown up in the same small town. Our parents attended high school together and worked at the same factory. I felt like Jada and I were close. I guess I was wrong. I was so gullible and naive, thinking everybody had my best interest at heart. Wrong, Wrong, Wrong! Wake up, Charlie.

Jada and I did exactly what she said we would that night. The baseball game was fun, but the birthday party was the best. I believe I did the electric slide, and this dance called the "He Man" all night.

At about midnight, Jada's mom picked us up. On the ride home, Jada and I laughed and recalled the favorable moments of the evening. However, once we pulled into the driveway of the house, Jada claimed to be sick. She told her mom that her stomach hurt, and she needed to go to bed. Once we were all inside, Jada's mom told us to take a bath before going to bed.

Jada pulled me in the bathroom to tell me what her true plans were.

"My godbrother and my boyfriend are about to come

over here. I need you to help me let the window u
can come in. My godbrother likes you, too, gul.

My face lit up. I wasn't the cutest thang. I had just
entered my awkward stage in life, so my confidence was
nonexistent. Being the naive child I was, I asked for
confirmation.

"Does he like me for real?"

"Yes, gul," Jada said, rolling her eyes this time.

"But I'm thirteen and he's seventeen. My mommy not
gonna let him be my boyfriend."

Rolling her eyes once again, Jada said, "Yo mommy
not gonna know. Have you ever *did it* before?"

"Did what?" I said, totally oblivious to what she was
indicating.

"Charlie, you a virgin with all that butt you got?"

"Yes, I talk to Jesus every day, and he said I gotta be
married to 'do it.'"

Jada replied, "Girl, Jesus don't talk to you. He is a
spirit, not a man. You can do it whenever you feel like it
if you love somebody. Shoot, I been doing it since I was
twelve. I'm totally fine. You should try it tonight with my
godbrother, Chauncey."

I looked more confused, scared, and really wanted my
daddy. All these awful thoughts played in my head. Geesh,
I was nervous. I knew I wasn't turning on Jesus to 'do it'
with a crush. I didn't love him. The thought of it gave me
the chills. However, I assisted Jada in helping the guys
in through the window. Once they were in, Jada made

peanut butter and jelly sandwiches and brought them to her room for us. As soon as the opportunity allowed, Jada lied and told her godbrother, Chauncey, I wanted to do it with him and that I loved him.

I was so taken aback by her comment. I was speechless for about two minutes. Jada and her boyfriend tiptoed into the guest bedroom, leaving Chauncey and me in her room.

I guess Chauncey was hungry, because he had two sandwiches, gobbling them down like the meal was the last supper. The more I looked at him and listened to him talk, the more I was convinced that he wasn't my crush after all. He was arrogant, cocky, a bit disrespectful, and just ugly … looking like a black grasshopper-wasp-bee mixture. He asked me was it true that I loved him.

"No," I answered.

"Do you like me, though?" Chauncey asked.

"Nope, I sure don't."

"You just scared, Mighty. I know you a virgin. I can tell."

"How can you tell?" I asked.

"The way you walk. The way you look. You're a good girl … ain't nobody been talking about you giving it up around here."

He paused for a moment before following up with, "Can I be your first?"

"No!" I boldly replied.

"I know you like me. I know you want to … you're just scared."

"No, I do not! I think you're ugly!" I said.

Moving close to me, Chauncey placed his hands over my mouth. "Shh … be quiet. If you make noise, you're going to wake up Jada's mom."

Suddenly, my body was frozen in fear.

He then gave me a hug and told me to relax. "I won't hurt you," he said.

I could hear my heart beating. He slowly rubbed my neck and kissed my cheeks between bites of his sandwich. Then, suddenly, he stuffed his half-eaten sandwich from his mouth into my mouth. "Shh … don't scream," he cautioned. I began to kick and attempt to fight him off me. Jada came in the room after hearing the tussle. All she did was look. She didn't do or say anything to Chauncey. She finally made eye contact with me and said, "You will be okay. Just be quiet."

I looked at Jada like, *Bitch, don't you see me fighting for my life?* I spit the sandwich in Chauncey's face.

His hands felt like a bed of nails piercing my side as he gripped my waist. With tears streaming down my face, I repeatedly begged him to stop.

I looked into his cold eyes right before he slapped me so hard that I hit the floor. "Shut the fuck up!" he yelled as he began to unbutton his pants.

I kicked him in his balls as hard as I could, causing him fall to his knees. I ran as fast as I could to the front of the house, yelling out to Ms. Richards. I was met with dead silence because Ms. Richards did not reply. Looking back over my shoulder, I could see Chauncey dragging down the hall after me. I bolted out the back door, never looking back. I ran the entire three blocks home without stopping, not even to catch my breath. To my surprise, when I turned the corner of my street, I spotted Ms. Richards' car parked in our driveway. It didn't take a genius to know why.

CHAPTER 4

This was the year I earned my degree in deceitfulness which later led to adultery. That entire rape experience taught me that people are faithful to no one but themselves. Within a twenty-four-hour period, I saw my father entertain two women during my mom's absence without shame or remorse. Carrying this experience into adulthood birthed the motto, "I will get a man before he gets me."

As a young adult, I mastered adultery. I mean, honestly, everybody cheats, right? We have all used someone or allowed ourselves to be used. At twenty-three I lacked maturity and a real role model of what marriage looks like. Marrying my daughter's father was the worst decision I made in my life. He was totally in love with our daughter. We named her Phoenix Sun after his favorite basketball team, but I referred to her most often as "Baby girl."

During one of those many difficult times during my marriage, it wasn't uncommon for me to watch people at Hollywood Bar and Grill. Sitting at the bar, with my fitted black bodycon dress, long, silky hair, yellow strappy stilettos, gold accessories, no make-up, just a light gloss on my lips, I tried hard to sit and mind my own business. Actually, I pretended not to notice him. As he walked past me, I could smell the Creed cologne dancing with his body chemistry, that perfectly tailored suit hugging his body, and the Italian-made shoes he wore. I wasn't sure if I had pissed my pants or if I had an orgasm at the sight of this man.

That little voice in my head said, *Ignore him. Turn around, Mighty. Face the bar and look at the television.* So, I did. The timer in my head began to count down … *5, 4, 3, 2, 1* … I could smell his cologne. He was standing behind me. *Don't move, Mighty.* The alarm in my head sounded … *Danger. Danger. Danger. Guard yourself. Don't do it.* But the other voice in my head said, *Guurrlll, he's fine. You're available to entertain him. Shiddddd, go for it!*

Before I could conceive another thought, I felt a tap on my shoulder.

"Excuse me. Are you here alone? If you are, you shouldn't be."

No words could exit my mouth. I just stared at him. Then, a warm smile plastered across my face. Turning to face him directly, before I could answer, this stranger gave me a dozen roses with a note written on a napkin. I unfolded the napkin and read the note: *I often see you here alone. Your energy excites me. I have taken care of your meal. Here's a little gift for your time. Oh, my name is Terrance. Call me.*

Wait a dayum minute. I was supposed to be the pimp here. Roses and a note, cool idea. Sure, I would call him, but he would have to wait at least two weeks. I had other things to do. I was the G.O.A.T in this playa game, partner. I was twenty-three years old and living my best life. I had a decent job, men taking care of me, and I was married to a deadbeat, good-for-nothing-but-fuckin'-up junky of a man named George.

Reflecting, I don't know why I married George to begin with. That lil' three-hundred and fifty thousand he received from his lawsuit wasn't worth me entering into a legally binding relationship with him. This notion that money was the cure all, was the biggest lie I told myself for years. The most damaging part was pretending that his recreational drug habit and emotional abuse were only temporary. Marrying a druggie led me to misery, I was willing to settle for any way out of this debacle of a marriage.

One thing for sure, George was obsessed with Phoenix and his sex was beyond what you could imagine. We had been married for eleven months, together off and on four years, and I regret every day of it. It would take strategy to leave him without him trying to kill me.

Getting home that evening, my estranged husband was sitting on my steps. As I approached him, he immediately began to yell. "Where is my daughter?" he said, his eyes piercing as though he could see right through me. Before I could respond, he went into the reason why he was really standing on my doorstep. "Why do you keep sending me these papers to sign? You ain't gone never get rid of me, bitch! I'mma keep fucking you good, and you're going to be right here with me."

Unfortunately for me, in the state of Virginia, we would have to be separated for twelve months before a divorce could be granted.

Two months after we said "I do," we split. I filed for a divorce. He was not pleased with my decision. He begged, cried, left notes, sent flowers to my job, went to rehab, got a new job, cried, beat on my door …you name it, he tried it all. But he couldn't keep me.

"You're pitiful, George," I said with disgust. "Go home or I'll call the police again."

"So! This my damn house, stupid hoe."

I hit him as hard as I could, knocking him off his feet. I tried to reach for the door to open it and get away from him, but he caught me, grabbed my hair and pulled me to the ground. He straddled me and began to slap me repeatedly. Upon hearing the commotion outside, my neighbors called the cops. Sadly, we both went to jail that night.

After George admitted to the police that the altercation was all his fault, they released me. This was a true blessing, because he had to sit in jail for six and half months.

About a week later, I called Terrance. When he

answered, I just started talking. "Hi, Terrance. This is Charlie … from the club. Remember me?"

"Charlie, I've been waiting on your call, girl. I almost forgot about you."

"Really, Terrance? How could you forget something you're waiting for?" I asked. He ignored the questions, like I knew he would. We talked for about thirty minutes and made plans to meet for dinner the upcoming Saturday. Where we were going on the date would be a surprise, he said. My radar really went up when he asked me for my full name and birthday. I gave him what he asked for with slight hesitation.

I was so excited about Saturday. I think I booked my week to make the time pass by quicker. When Saturday finally arrived, I took my daughter out for breakfast and to the nail salon. I explained to her that she will get a chance to stay overnight with her best friend. She was super excited that she jumped up and gave me a big hug and kiss. Besides, her best friend's mom was my best friend. I felt safe with her there. I never ever allowed her to stay with anyone besides her father and his family. I knew she would be well taken care of by them.

After dropping off my little princess, I hurried home. At 6:45 that evening, my doorbell rang. To my surprise, Terrance had sent a car to pick me up. I stood in the door flabbergasted. Then the driver took my hand to assist me down the stairs to the car. Upon entering the car, the driver passed me a note that read: *Miss Mighty, tonight will be the night you will fall in love. I hope you grabbed an overnight bag. I want to show you something.*

I politely handed the note back to the driver and said, "Well, let's go." I figured that if I needed overnight essentials, Terrance could buy them for me, including the bag itself.

The black-on-black Bentley had twenty-three white roses, nineteen red roses, and three yellow roses spread across the seats. During the drive, the driver stated he had never known Mr. Miller, a.k.a. Terrance, to be so extravagant with any woman, so I must've been special. I rolled my eyes. I'd heard that line before. About five minutes later, we arrived at Sims Miller Private Airport. My eyes grew wider than a deer in headlights. I looked at the driver and asked the dumbest question. "Are we having dinner on a helipad?"

He chuckled. No, ma'am. Mr. Miller is waiting for you."

When I exited the car, the driver handed me another note. I carefully unfolded the piece of paper. He said my real name this time.

> *Charlie, I knew from the first time I saw you sitting at Hollywood Bar and Grill two years ago that this day would come. I would finally get an opportunity to take you out on a date. I'm looking for many*

more dates with you. Yes, another rose for
a rose.

Kisses,
Terrance

The stewardess escorted me to the aircraft. After being seated on the plane, Terrance kissed my forehead. "How was your evening, Charlie?

"Fine."

"Where is your overnight bag?"

"Where are we going, Terrance Miller? And why do I need an overnight bag for dinner?"

He sighed deeply and chuckled. "Don't give me a hard time. We're flying to Atlanta for dinner to meet up with a few of my close friends. I thought I would surprise you, but you're making this a little difficult."

Wait, sir, a flight? For dinner? I was elated and at the same time scared. "How do I know you're not plotting to kill me or kidnap me or sell me to the underground sex trade" I joked, feeling tense.

"Charlie, would you be here if you thought any of that?"

"I might be … I might be a dare devil. I'm glad I brought Mr. Wesson Smith with me."

"Who?" Terrance asked, puzzled.

"My gun. I don't know you or your intentions," I said, patting the side of my purse.

Terrance chuckled and didn't flinch. "Charlie, buckle your seat belt, sweetheart, and prepare for takeoff."

Oh my! The restaurant deserved a ten-star rating. The food danced on my palate and my waistline. The evening was beyond amazing. I was equally impressed with the lodging. I had never had a butler, maid, nor driver. I felt myself panicking inwardly. *What have I gotten myself into?* After a long, hot shower, there were more damn rose petals leading to the bedroom. And what did I find? You guessed it ... another damn note.

> *I will return shortly. If you don't love me by*
> *now, you will. I feel like I love you already.*

I wasn't impressed with the note. In my world, I didn't love no man. Ever.

About two o'clock that morning, I was awakened by music playing. It was the soulful voice of a new artist ... Jill Scott. I was also awakened to find his head between my legs. He ate my pussy for about an hour. I know I nutted about five times. Nibbling on my nipples, licking my neck, pulling my hair, he said, "Are you ready?"

I was so weak at this point, I couldn't move, speak,

or mumble. I felt as though I should've been forewarned. Not one smoke signal went off, no red flags, nor my inner woman said anything. It was like I was being set up to be punished.

Terrance looked into my eyes, staring deep into my soul. "Are you ready to fall in love with my tongue game?"

"What does that mean Terrance?"

"I can show you better than I can tell you, Charlie." He commenced to playing with my pussy … licking and creaming it before putting that monster of a dick inside me. He slowly slid the head in. There was just enough friction and vibration to force the rest of the elephant trunk inside me. I felt like my body split in half. I couldn't take it. I must have screamed to the top of my lungs.

I recall promising myself then and there, after this relation, big penises were gonna be a "no" for me. My cream pie couldn't take it nor my nerves. I ended up calling my mom, crying and complaining, wondering why the lips of my vagina were swollen as if they had been sucked into a bottle. She laughed so hard … that hard laugh … that grasping for air kinda laugh. Then she explained.

"Honey, that's what they call the cherry being popped. Ever heard of that?"

I had … when I was a little girl. It was a saying the older folks uttered quite often, especially when they wanted to warn the little girls about boys or men, for that matter, who had "real" sex with girls for the first time.

"Oh," I said. I guess it made sense.

Awakened by the morning sun kissing my cheeks, a slight smile fancied my face. More gifts and more fuckin' roses greeted me. I hated roses, by the way. An immediate urge to urinate took my attention from the gifts and ugly roses. I could feel the warm urine running down my leg as I rushed to the toilet. As I turned on the shower, I heard a deep, strong voice, which caught me by surprise

"Good morning, Charlie. Did I startle you?" he asked.

"No, you scared the hell out of me!" I said as I began to undress.

"I see you haven't opened your gifts."

"No, Mr. Miller, I haven't. Where have you been?" I asked.

"Charlie, you don't open my gifts; you don't say thank you; you're questioning my whereabouts, all before giving me a good morning kiss."

I rolled my eyes. Terrance chuckled. "May I join you in the shower, Charlie?"

"Only If you do not try anything with me. I'm in pain."

"No?" Terrance said with a smirk on his face.

"Noooo," I screamed. "I can't take any more of you inside me." We both looked at each other eye to eye, seemingly for hours, but in reality, ten seconds. As I bit my lip, we both burst into laughter and jumped into the shower … together. The shower was long and pleasant. Double shower heads, a shower bench, and soft, boring elevator music played as he babbled about his future plans. Mr. Miller shared with me his meeting schedule, our dinner plans, and once again, questioned why I hadn't opened the gifts.

"Mr. Miller, I'll open the gifts on one condition."

"What's that, Charlie?"

"If you promise to spoil me with the things that I like versus what you want me to have." Before he could answer, the doorbell rang.

"I'm going to make you eat those words, Charlie. I want more for you than you want for yourself," he said as he jumped out of the shower and wrapped a towel around his naked body.

I tried my best to hear the conversation, but the loud music drowned out the deep voices coming from the front room. But as I listened a little more intently, I detected a woman's voice. *Did he just tell her to calm down … that he will see her tonight?* What the hell! *Did he forget I was in here?*

Leaving the shower running, I crept out of the bathroom to peep around the corner, just in enough time to see this negro kiss some woman on her forehead and give her a goodbye hug.

"I love you," she said.

"I love you too," he replied.

I was pissed. Fumes were coming from my ears. Did he really just hug her and kiss the forehead of a chick who appeared to be every bit of twenty-one years old?

"Charlie, what are you doing in there?" Terrance yelled out to me. I guess he no longer heard me bumping around in the shower.

"Who's at the door?" I said, turning the shower water off.

Terrance came back into the bathroom wearing a big grin on this face. "You sound jealous. Why do you want to know, Charlie?"

I shrugged. "Okay, Mr. Miller, let's not play this game."

"If you open the gifts, you will know."

I felt it coming. I was about to explode with anger. I tried to stop it. Before I knew it, it all came out at once. "Bushwhacker, I know you don't have another bitch coming to our hotel room, looking for you while you're with me." I was heated. This negro had fumes coming out of my head now, not just my ears.

He turned around and headed for the bedroom. I followed. "Say that again for me, please?" he said.

"I said, I just know you ain't got a female coming up here to our hotel room."

Terrance fell back on the bed in laughter. "Do I sense an emotion from *Ms. Charlie*?" Sitting up, he grabbed my thin frame, threw me across the bed, and held me down. Staring into my eyes, he said, "I love you, Charlie MacClemore. That's the only promise I can give you right now, and I hope you will love me back. Now, open the gifts so we can go, lil lady."

I felt an unfamiliar sense of helplessness and a strange

sense of comfort and protection as he held me. I completely loved it. As I looked around, I saw three more boxes, a hanging bag, and another bouquet of roses. I felt myself getting anxious. The boxes were beautifully wrapped in pink, gold, and silver paper. I grabbed the first box. The attached card read, *A little something to make you dance.* Inside were a pair of gold Versace shoes. In the second box, was a black Donna Karan dress. In the third box was a pair of beautiful earrings. Every box had a handwritten note attached to the enclosed gift.

I opened the last box and closed it back real fast. *He must've given me the wrong box*, I thought.

"Open the box, girl. Don't be afraid of it," Terrance said, scanning the expression on my face.

Slightly tilting my head to the side with a puzzled look, I mumbled, "What is this?"

"Go ahead … open the box," he encouraged.

I slowly reopened the box. It was still there. So shiny and big. Terrance took it upon himself to take the gift out of the box for me.

"Here. Take it. It's yours," he said, handing it to me.

"So heavy and shiny," was all I could say. Then I noticed the price tag. My eyes nearly popped out of my head.

He grabbed the sparkling piece of jewelry from me, holding my right hand. "Charlie, I promise to love you for eternity. Please accept this ring as an acceptance of my commitment to you."

I was completely speechless.

"Are you going to answer me, Charlie?" he said, realizing I was still mesmerized by the ring that I hadn't given him any type of response.

"I accept," I mumbled. I mean, how could I refuse?

A few weeks later, Phoenix and I were at Terrance's place prepping for a cookout when my daughter called out to me. "Mommy, your phone's ringing. It's Daddy again." I abruptly answered the phone. "What do you want, George?"

His voice was raspy and seductive, causing chills to run up and down my spine. "Hey, my Charlie's Angel."

I hated when he called me that. I was no angel of his.

He then dropped the bomb on me … the words I didn't miss nor want to hear. "Baby, I'm sorry. I promise I will be a better husband to you. Due to good behavior, I'll be home in five days."

A long period of silence that seemed like eternity passed.

"Baby, are you there? Did you hear what I said? I will be home in five days. It'll be just Phoenix, you, and me … one big happy family again. This time, I promise to treat you right … shower you with love."

I zoned out. All I could hear was "blah blah blah." Empty promises once again. Words wouldn't form in my mouth.

"Baby, say something," George begged. "Baby the phone is about to disconnect in two minutes."

By this time, I had made up my mind. Time was up. I disconnected the call. When I looked up, I saw Phoenix waiting at the door, smiling with anticipation, asking a string of questions. "Is Daddy coming home, Mommy? Is he, Mommy? Is Daddy coming home? Are you going to tell him about Mr. Miller? Is Mr. Miller going to be nice to you? Do you think Daddy and Mr. Miller are going to fight over you? Granny K said she is gonna tell Daddy about Mr. Miller, so Daddy can whip you and him."

Granny K was my nosy-ass mother-in-law who was always in our business. If she would have allowed her son to be a man and not stay stuck up under her sucking her titty, he would have been a real man, a good husband and a good father. But he was none of these.

Now, what are we going to do? I thought. I knew I was going to have to concoct some type of sad sob story. *I have to tell Mr. Miller. I have to move. I have to file for this divorce.* My head began to throb. I only had five days to move, file for a divorce, convince Mr. Miller to pay for the divorce, change my identity, and become a ghost, so George wouldn't kill me! Just the thought alone caused me to sweat profusely.

I had to get ahold of myself ... my running emotions. *Think this thing through, Charlie. You got this. Call your best friend.* That's what I decided to do ... have a girl-friends' meeting of the minds. I needed an immediate resolve. I paged my girlfriends' group 911. All my girls knew the meet-up time and place.

When I pulled up to Regay's house, she was standing outside awaiting my arrival.

"Regay, I'm so nervous," I said, getting out of the car. I was going right into the dilemma.

There was no sugar coating it.

Regay called Christina. Christina called Missy, and Missy called Sonya. Before I knew it, all my friends were at my rescue … to help me make a crucial decision in my life. Each of these women played a special role. Regay was my "down for whatever" friend. Christina was my let's kill every man in America that hurt a black woman friend. Missy was my praying friend. And Sonya was the rational and logical friend.

I was like, *Dayumm, how did you all beat me here?*

"Girl, what happened this time. What man are you running from now?" Sonya asked all in one sentence.

George will be released from jail in five days.

"Whew, girl, that man is going to kill you," Regay blurted out.

"Please, let's talk before you begin your judgement and crucify commentary Regay," I said. "Besides, I have practically moved in with Terrance. He has met Phoenix and we're considering —" I stopped in the middle of my sentence.

"Considering what?" the four of them said in unison.

"Mighty, what are you considering, besides making another bad decision?" Sonya said with her arms folded.

I blurted it out in one breath. "Okay, I told Terrance yes to the ring. It's not a formal engagement type of thing ... just a commitment ring. I allowed him to meet Phoenix ... and I'm afraid George will kill us both. He's just that jealous and determined that he's coming home to me ... us," I said, exhaling a deep breath.

A thunder of laughter engulfed the room.

"Girl, we thought you were about to die. Charlie ... Miss Mighty ... you know better than we do. Aren't you the self-proclaimed female pimp?" smart-mouthed Regay felt the need to say.

Christina cussed everybody out on my behalf, right before turning to me to help me devise a master plan to get rid of George for good and disappear for good too.

Regay's eyes widened. "Why should we help Charlie this time?"

Missy rolled her neck and turned to Regay. "She just said they're letting George out in five days ... In other words, he'll be a free man. You know George is crazy. He will kill her without hesitation once he finds out about Charlie and Terrance."

All four of my friends sat in silence for a moment. "This shit ain't funny. Help me, bitches,"

I said. "Y'all always got some shit to say, but I see none of y'all ain't got anything to say now. Won't even offer for me to come stay at y'all's place. I get it," I said, clasping my hands together.

"I have an idea," Sonya said. "Tell Miller what he needs to hear to make it all go away.

"Like what, Sonya? What should I say? My emotions are getting the best of me, friend, and I can't think."

"I paused, biting my nails as I pondered the idea. She was right. In this case, honesty was the best policy.

My heart raced as I waited for Terrance to answer the call. He answered on the fourth ring.

"Hey, babe," he greeted.

"Hey," I replied.

"What's wrong? You don't sound like yourself," he said, detecting the nervousness in my voice.

"I don't want to bother you, but—"

"But nothing, Charlie. What's wrong?" Terrance asked in a firm tone.

After explaining to Mr. Miller how I felt my life was in danger with George, the next day, the movers were at my place. Terrance moved me to a condominium on the beach. Gave me the key, told me to sign the lease paperwork at my convenience. What the hell? I had a four p.m. appointment with an attorney to discuss the divorce. He had it all mapped out to make sure everything was conducive to my work schedule and Phoenix's needs.

I was so impressed and felt loved, but my gut was

telling me something different. I knew something was off with this fella, but I couldn't quite put my hands on it. After speaking to the attorney, he assured me the divorce was in my favor. My soon-to-be ex hated me, but Terrance guaranteed me George wouldn't fight me on anything.

With a puzzled look on my face, I asked, "Terrance, how do you know George is not going to fight me in court? He is a bad husband but a great father. I don't see him allowing this to be an easy case."

"Charlie, I run this city. Trust me; in court tomorrow you will get exactly what you want."

"Court tomorrow ... Wait, how did you pull that off and get George to agree to appear in court, Terrance?"

"Charlie, hush and trust me, okay!"

We showed up at *William Jake's Courthouse* in Portsmouth, Va at nine o'clock a.m. I was divorced at nine fifteen am. George said nothing the whole time we were there. He didn't look my way. I guess we could move on with life casually, with no hard feelings.

In the back of my mind, I wondered whether Terrance had confronted George and threatened him because George was acting strange. I was now scared for both of our lives.

The day of the divorce, Terrance and I celebrated over dinner with friends and family. Terrance took us to this member's only exclusive six-star dining hall. It was an astounding venue. My friends were intimidated. After the four courses, the concierge asked for all the guests to be moved into a private dining area.

The private area was something to behold. There was an orchestra, candles, wine, and both red and white roses covered the floor. It was beautiful. Everyone gathered at the table to be served dessert. My friends and I were all so shocked and bewildered, I couldn't enjoy my food due to the breathtaking ambiance.

After everyone had their dessert, the music changed a slight bit. We were all dancing, drinking, and having a ton of fun. I was dancing and laughing so hard, I didn't notice my mom and brothers had walked in. I heard a tapping of the glass. Mr. Miller was requesting everyone's attention be directed to the big screen. I burst into tears as my mommy and brothers walked toward me. I was so excited to see her and feel her hugs. She whispered in my ear, "Make whatever decision you want, baby girl. No is an option."

I was like, *Huh?* She grabbed me closer and said, "Shhhhh … just trust me." We exchanged "I love yous" several times. Then a short film began, a beautiful, picturesque dissertation of how Mr. Miller and I met. I was so caught up that when I tried to turn around, my body wouldn't move. Terrance's sister pointed down. There Terrance was on bended knee with another six-karat diamond ring, confessing his eternal love for me.

I just got divorced. Why would you put me through all that hell again, being insensitive to my healing process, and ignore the fact that I'm not in love with you? It was the perfect engagement, so how could I say no? I couldn't. I didn't have the gall to say no. So, what I did was pretend to faint. Yes, honey chile, I fainted on purpose. I called myself scanning the room, attempting to plan the fall without seriously hurting myself. However, my clumsy butt hit the corner of the table and knocked myself out for real for real.

I woke up in a hospital bed with an IV in my arm and a bandage wrapped around my head. There were close to twenty people in my hospital room staring at me. Terrance's big, tall, sexy self was right in the bed with me. I stared at him and noticed some things about him. I saw the spirit of compassion and generosity. He was so sweet, as much as I wanted to go with the flow, something was holding me back. *What is it he isn't telling me?*

Moments later, the doctor who had been attending to me walked in. "Miss MacClemore," he said, calling me by my maiden name. "I'm Dr. Jones. Are you aware you have been in the hospital for two weeks and your husband hasn't left your side, along with a very supportive group of friends and family? I always wished to have a family and friends like these. You must be one special person."

"Wait, husband? Two weeks?" I said, dumbfounded.

"Yes, two weeks. Your husband hasn't left your side. As a matter of fact, he and I have even had coffee together."

"Everybody out, except you, Terrance and Dr. Jones." I was confused, irritated, and upset. "And you nutcrackers better be honest. Are y'all sleeping together?!" The last time I'd seen Ralph, now Dr. Jones, he was introducing me to a man named Timothy that he said he was going to marry.

Terrance frowned.

"Answer me, dammit!" I demanded.

"Charlie, calm down. How hard did you hit your head?" Terrance said.

"I need answers, Ralph!" Ralph's face turned blue. "Ralph, where is your husband? And when did you become a doctor?"

"No, baby, Dr. Ralph is married to a woman. She's a sweetie and she's expecting. I have gotten the opportunity to meet with them both. We discussed property purchases and his medical background and family. You know I wouldn't allow just anyone to be your doctor. Dr. Ralph Jones has passed the test."

So, Ralph, you want me to believe you're a doctor. You also want me to believe you're married to a woman? Get the fuck out here with that. Anyway ...

"Well, what's wrong with me then? Why have I been here for two weeks?"

"You suffered a major blow to the head. We had to put you in an induced coma," Dr. Jones said.

"Am I better now?"

"Yes, but you have to calm down. We need to talk to you about the recovery process." I saw his mouth moving but heard no sound. Pulling back the covers, Ralph began to rub my legs ... but I felt nothing.

"Charlie, do you hear me?" Dr. Jones said.

"Why do I not have feeling in my legs? What is wrong with me?"

"Well, as I was starting to explain … I had to place a tap in your lower back to minimize the risk of any further injury. We will be removing the tap today. You should have the feeling back in your lower extremities within a few hours. However, you will have to take it easy. I'll have the nurse to bring up the orders and see you in a few hours. I … I have to go complete my rounds. But I'll be back to check on you," Ralph said, excusing himself from the uncomfortable conversation.

"Thank you, Dr. Fake Ralph Jones."

"You're welcome, Ms. MacClemore."

"Nice seeing you, Doc," said Terrance Miller. "Charlie, that was rude for you to treat Dr. Jones that way. Why did you say those things, Charlie?"

Ignoring his question, I asked my own. "Why do I have this ring on my finger, Terrance?

"Because you said yes."

"When did I say yes?" I challenged.

Terrance didn't answer, just sort of gave me that "You did, and ain't shit you can do about it" look.

"Terrance, I can't marry you. I just got a divorce. I need time to heal to get to know me again. I have a daughter. Where is my child, by the way? Has she come to see me? I want to see her."

"She's with her father. Yes, they both have come every

day. She prayed for you every day. I got an opportunity to speak to your ex-husband about us. I had to apologize for sending my guys to rough him a bit about divorcing you, letting him know you are mine. He was not pleased with our relationship, but after I paid him ten grand to stop harassing you, he has been good … even kind of pleasant."

"Terrance, you can't go around buying people off, threatening people, and you can't buy me. I'm not marrying you."

"Yes, you are, Charlie … and I'll wait six months, a year, or two years. I'll wait for you."

He just didn't get it. I had no intentions on marrying him.

"Can you have my friends and family come back to the room, please?"

Terrance ushered my family and friends into the room. In came Phoenix, running with flowers and a handwritten card. I was so happy to see her. Before I could read the entire card, Tasha, Terrance's assistant, walked in.

"Why are you here, Tasha?"

"I've tried to call several times, to no avail."

"Don't you think it was a reason for that? Terrance get your lil' fake assistant out of my room, and you can go with her." I said, focusing my attention back to my daughter and her handwritten card.

Tasha was pissed, but I did not care. She had a folder in her hand. "Miss or Mrs. Charlie, you'll want to read this before I go."

"What is it, Tasha?" I said as I snatched the folder from her. Once I opened the letter, my heart skipped several beats. I became hot; tears were flowing out of nowhere. Inside the folder was a sealed letter from my attorney.

"Miss Charlie Rose MacClemore has been accused of breaking into a capital two server and gaining access to over 100,000 social security numbers and bank accounts, plus an undisclosed number of people's names, addresses, and credit scores. Charges have been filed on behalf of BonTon Bank and the U.S. Department of Justice.

"Is this real?" I asked, looking at Terrance. I asked him succinctly, "Terrance, why does she have these documents? Who are you? What are you trying to do to me? I'm a mother, a daughter, an aunt, a friend. My people need me."

"I … I had no clue you'd be caught up in this. This was my mess. But don't worry. I'm gonna get you the best attorney money can buy."

"Best attorneys, Terrance? Why? I haven't done anything."

I passed the documents to my mom. She scanned them and burst into tears. I slid under the sheets and screamed to the top of my lungs.

How could they have a warrant for my arrest for fraud and embezzlement? Terrance did this to me, and he was going to pay the price for it!

CHAPTER 5

*D*eception—the act of causing someone to believe something that is false as true or valid.

TLC's infamous song, "What about Your Friends" started blasting. I listened intently to the words. I had no clue about what a friend was or if I was really a friend. I believed everything someone told me who I thought was a friend. If the next person told me something different, I would believe that too. I wondered why no one taught me how to be a friend or to have my own mind as a child.

At fifteen years old, I called myself dating this guy named Damon. I was a virgin … so naïve and gullible. He was kind of a cornball himself. If I had any type of sense then, I would have changed the "a" to an "e" and called him by his real name—Demon. He sure fooled me. All that sweet talk, being nice, being smart, serving in the community, going to church every Sunday, being an after-school tutor, the teacher's pet, and whatever else …

none of it meant anything. He was sexy in his own way. I will admit he wasn't the best-looking fella, but he had me, so looks didn't matter. I made him look good. That was my thinking at the time … me and my dumb self.

Damon was a year ahead of me in school. An honor student, had a car, was somewhat popular, and his sense of humor was what got me. He protected me and made me laugh. Damon and I dated for two years before we even thought about tongue kissing. He was a gentleman at all times … in the beginning, that is. He always supported me and listened to me gripe and complain about how horrible my life was, when in fact, it was typical teenage life. I had no real complaints when I looked back on my life as a teen.

Damon told me horror stories of how cruel and mean his mom was. She would put him on punishment at seventeen years old if he didn't take out the trash, kiss her good night, wash the cars, mop, do the dishes, rake the yard, you name it. He never really liked me to come over to his house. I swear his mom practiced witchcraft. She hated me and would tell me to not call or come over whenever he was on punishment, claiming it was all my fault.

When I did reluctantly come over, she would burn some type of concoction and would smear black ashes over her face along with candles and weird prayers. After seeing that, I couldn't figure out why he wasn't crazy too. He would always tell me when he left for college, he would only come home to see me. How he loved his mom, but his home life was miserable. I would try to get him to give me more information, but he said he didn't want to scare me off.

It was approaching spring break. Damon and I had a mutual friend we were both close to. She said Damon had been asking about having sex with me. We had been together for over two years and wanted to take it to the next level. I was wondering why he didn't just ask me about it. She said he was afraid and didn't want to offend me or didn't want me to break up with him.

Now, my mother had warned me to not trust this gal. Her name was Alicia Beckams. She was one of the first kids I met in elementary school. In school, a group of us would hang together. Vickie, Jasmin, Tiffany, Nina, Khloe, Shanti, Rhonda, Alicia, and me. I favored Vickie and Khloe more out of the group. Vickie and Khloe were best friends. They were chill and laid back and respected each other. During our junior year, we were all preparing for a big Spring Break trip to Mexico. It was considered an all-class trip, both junior and senior classes from all surrounding schools. The trip was sure to be epic. We were all excited about all the rival schools joining forces to vacation together. One of my favorite teachers, Mrs. DeJarnett, and her bestie were two of the twenty chaperones. Mrs. DeJarnett also warned me about Damon. She told me he was evil like his mommy and to not ignore the signs. She told me I was mistaking puppy love for real love. "Charlie, Damon is controlling and manipulating. Pay attention to the red flags."

I thanked her for sharing her thoughts with me, but my mind was made up. I loved him.

The day had come. My mommy was so nervous for me to travel abroad without her. My mommy was very protective of me. It took her months to tell me yes for this trip. I believe we had over a hundred hours of drills on safety and another thousand-hour talks about who my real friends were. Finally, I said, "I get it, Mommy ... I will call you three times a day. I will make sure I watch my friends, and I will make sure Damon and I don't have sex.

Our talk was interrupted by the phone ringing.

"Hello?"

It was Alicia. "Hi Charlie ... or should I say Mighty? I have condoms for you and Damon. Are you ready?"

Untangling the long phone cord to walk away from my mom, I whispered, "Why are you trying to pressure me to have sex with Damon, Alicia? Is it because you are no longer a virgin and want me to not be one?"

Alicia immediately got defensive. "I was just trying to be your friend ... tryna look out for you," Alicia replied.

"If I have to explain it to you, Alicia, I don't consider that being a friend. I told you I wasn't ready to have sex yet."

"We will all be with our boyfriends, and I didn't want to leave you out. I just want you to know I have your back."

"I don't need you to have my back by coercing me to have sex. I need you to be a real friend and respect my wishes."

"Where is all of this coming from, Charlie? I know you and Damon been through some stuff. Has he hit you again? I know the last time you said he apologized and said he won't do it again. Did you tell your mom?"

I replied, "No, I didn't tell her, and he didn't hit me. He pushed me because I overreacted. He quickly helped me up and apologized. He explained he sometimes reacts because his mommy is so mean and does the same thing. He doesn't want his girlfriend to react that way. But why are you deflecting?"

"I'm not, Charlie. You are just acting weird, like I don't talk to you about sex all the time."

"He had a hard time dealing with his mother's behavior due to her divorce from his dad. Besides, I have never told you I want to have sex. Leave that conversation alone, please," I said, defending Damon. Then it dawned on me, and I didn't comment further. Damon's business was not her business.

Once we arrived at school, all the students were assigned chaperones and bus numbers.

Mr. Jasper came rushing on the bus, breathing hard and calling out our names with such aggression and bitterness. I think he hated his job. Mr. Jasper was our vice principal, who did not play at all, by any means. He yelled at us, cussed, and told our parents he didn't give a damn about feelings, that he was there to educate. Mr. Jasper was my friend, Karen's, stepdad. She was always embarrassed when he came around. He had a whistle he'd blow when trying to get students' attention. When he'd blow it, his spit would fly all over the place, including in our faces. We hated the sight of him and his darn whistle.

"Miss Goodie-Two-Shoes Charlie. You and all your little crew bring your asses to the front of the bus."

"Why, Mr. Jasper?" I asked.

"Because Miss Rosa Parks didn't fight for you to be in the back. As for you and your crew, y'all's little asses will be right up here with me and these other sorry-ass teachers."

He was so rude, but no one took him seriously. Mr. Jasper was so sweet and a giver. He worked hard for us to be able to accomplish our goals and, of course, go on this trip.

It was a long ride and draining flight to Cancun, Mexico. We all were given the rules as our teachers and VP held us hostage in the lobby of the hotel. I was perplexed at how many security guards surrounded us and the strict rules that applied and the limitations. I was grateful for the high-tech security, but why bring kids to a place where we couldn't have fun?

That damn whistle blew one more time. "Charlie, are you listening? You are the smallest little thang out here, ninety-five pounds soaking wet. You need to be listening and pay attention to these rules and get out that boy face."

I was so goofy, I laughed at him. Yes, sir ... yes, big sir," I joked.

He shook his head at me. "Keep an eye on her. She lacks common sense," he told everyone.

I smirked, under my breath, calling him an asshole.

After he released everyone to go prepare for dinner, Mr. Jasper asked Karen, Alicia, and me to stay behind to help with set-up.

"Charlie, come here."

Sir?

"I've been told that Damon has pushed, slapped, hit, or punched you. Is that true?"

Biting my lip and looking down, I replied, "No, sir."

"Charlie, don't lie to me. If he has, you need to let me know."

"No, Mr. Jasper, he hasn't. I promise." I was still lying, and he knew it.

"If you have any problems with him on this trip, you betta let me or another adult know. Don't be stupid, letting an ole knuckle-head boy put his hands on you."

We were having more fun than I expected on the trip, with only two more days before we were to head back home.

At the pool, there was a little guy, who appeared to be half Mexican and half black, flirting with me. I don't know if it was his curly hair, his sun-kissed skin, or his perfect smile that made me feel all warm on the inside. If I had to guess, I'd say he was definitely older than me by his disposition and overall conversation. He was so freakin' cute.

Damon noticed the attention I gave the guy, and his jealousy took over.

"You must wanna break up or something," he said, confronting me.

"What are you talking about?" I said, abruptly ending the conversation with the cute stranger.

"You're all giggles and smiles with this dude like you ain't got a boyfriend. You playing me for a fool in front of all these people."

"Look, Damon, don't be silly. This guy lives here and works here. He's just being nice, super nice actually, and hasn't disrespected me, like you sometimes do."

"Like I said … you must don't want a relationship, at least not with me."

"Damon didn't say anything when Maria asked to rub your back or you guys were playing in the pool. So, don't get mad at me for being friendly," I shot back. It felt good giving him a little taste of his own medicine.

He looked at me with fire in his eyes. I could tell he was pissed. But he couldn't respond how he wanted to. Everyone pretended to not notice his idiotic behavior, causing a scene by asking all those questions, showing his insecurity. He became furious. I walked away from our group of friends, with Damon in hot pursuit behind me. As I entered my hotel room, he immediately grabbed me and began to punch me as hard as he could, repeating, "I told you not to talk to him, didn't I? I told you not to look at him, didn't I? Why do you keep on insisting on playing me like a fool?!" His punches kept landing on me one after the other. Then, he slapped me so hard that I slammed into the wall and then hit the floor.

One of Damon's friends, Anthony, entered the room. He had a suspicion of what was probably going on. He closed the door and pulled Damon off me.

"Damon, what are you doing?! You could really hurt her and go to jail."

Anthony ran into the bathroom. I heard the water running, and before I knew it, he was placing wet towels over my eye. I caught a glimpse of Damon, who was nervously pacing the floor now, looking as though he didn't know what he had done. He was in a daze.

"What happened to her?"

Anthony replied, "You did this, man. Her face is covered with blood. Her eyes are all jacked up. What the fuck is wrong with you?"

Damon fell to the floor, sobbing. Then, when he had gathered himself together, he looked at me with a vicious stare and uttered the words that changed my perception of innocence versus guilt—"It's your fault this happened, Charlie. You made me do it, and you deserved it."

Just like that … My first "real" boyfriend placed a quilt of deception over my eyes.

CHAPTER 6

*D*amon's ambiguous remarks almost deprived me of valuing myself ... knowing my self-worth. As an adult, I realized this childhood experience shaped the way I dealt with men or, should I say, taught me to pay attention to the red flags and not ignore them.

As a grown woman, however, the spirit of deception played a huge role in my life. Ever since these types of incidents with Franko and Damon happened to me, my motto has been, "I'll get you before you get me," and I meant all of that.

After watching the movie, *Girl Six*. I decided to create an alter ego to make extra money. Multiple streams of income never hurt anybody. The job was easy enough. Answer calls, talk nasty, and secure my bag.

"Thank you for calling Delilah's Love Line. What's popping, daddy?" I knew exactly who it was calling. Like clockwork, my regular dirty John called every Wednesday night at 9:05 pm on his ride home from work. There wasn't anything special about him, not even his name. They were all called "Dirty Johns."

"Delilah, I miss that pretty voice of yours, ma'am."

"Hello, Boseman, I miss you too. How much time do you have tonight?" I said, trying to sound super sexy.

"Aww baby, I'm all yours tonight. We can be dirty as long as you want. I'm home alone."

"Oh, really, Boseman? How did that happen?"

"Well, she left me. She said I wasn't satisfying her in bed anymore. Plus, she doesn't want any more kids. She had a whole list of complaints. So, she left," he replied callously.

"What about the children?" I asked, not sure they had any.

"Well, you know we only have one child, right?"

"No, I didn't know that."

"Yep, just one."

"I guess you weren't lying about being unhappy," I said.

"Why would I lie?"

"Why do men lie about their unhappiness in a marriage? To get outside pussy."

"Not me."

"That's what they all say. But you're on the phone talking dirty to me."

"What do you think I'm supposed to do when she's around town poppin' her coochie with other men?"

I could hear the irritation in his voice. My money was at stake, so I changed the subject ... let him know I was on his side. "Boseman, did you ever tell her you found out she was sleeping with your best friend?"

"Naw, she didn't need to know that. I'm saving that for the custody battle. My daughter cried like crazy when she had to leave me. That really hurt, Delilah. But hey, enough about me."

"Are you ready to get naughty, Big Daddy Boseman?" I said, trying to disguise my voice with one of excitement.

I hated playing phone sex. I was sitting on the sofa, taking my breads down, but here he came calling, wanting me to talk sweet and sexy to him. It made me mad. I guessed it made him feel like a man ... and it paid the bills for me. I figured it was a better alternative than being a call girl and having to perform physical acts. Eww ... just the thought of it made me want to vomit.

"No, no, Delilah! You know we're friends now. It's been two years, and I don't know what you look like or what's your favorite food. Let's do something different besides you making me jack off every Wednesday."

I was glad he wanted to change the subject, and I was eager to answer the question. "Well, Boseman, I'm a single mom of one. I have a daughter also. She attends private school. By day, I am a licensed counselor. I work in the Flat Bush School District." I lied about where I worked just in case he tried to tell my business or find me. "What else do you want to know?" I added.

"Can I meet you?" he said?

"Meet me, as in face to face?"

"Yes, Delilah. I think I supplement your income well, and I deserve to meet you."

"Well, Boseman, you're paying for a service. And no, you can't meet me, and I am not interested in meeting you." I realized that was his abandonment and rejection talking based on the personal information he shared during our late-night calls. "You don't want to meet me."

"Why not, Delilah? I know what you do as a second income. You gotta pay for that baby's private school and designer shoes. One thing's for sure, I know you not sleeping with the men you be sex talking to, because I was one of your first clients, and you ain't never tried to see me."

Boseman was funny for thinking he could pay to meet me. That wasn't a part of the service I provided. I worked on a recorded love line for a reason; it was a substitute for prostitution on the streets. My line was only open from eight p.m. until midnight, Wednesday through Saturday. It was the easiest two dollars a minute a girl could make. But seemingly, Boseman was unaware of the background check or screening requirements on all regular callers. I needed to know who and what I was getting myself into.

He and one of my regular callers, tripped me out with the code switching. I wasn't a lil' hood girl; my parents gave me all the game to the streets, including Wall Street. I was no longer anybody's fool.

Boseman's portfolio would blow the average person away. He was a multi-millionaire, as the owner of Avery Productile. He had commercial property in the UAE as well as Africa. I also knew Boseman was his middle name. His government name was Ian Boseman Manning. I just played along with him to get along with him. Might I add, the man was very handsome, according to his LinkedIn profile picture.

"Delilah, why are you afraid to meet me? I'm a gentleman. I will take you somewhere nice. If you don't like me when you meet me, I won't call you anymore," he negotiated.

"No, Boseman, I don't do that. It's a conflict of interest. Besides, I don't know you."

"Delilah, you know more about me than I know about me, all those questions you ask," he said with a slight chuckle.

Boseman and I stayed on the phone until about four o'clock in the morning. I guess we were friends. He finally let his guard down and began to tell me about his childhood and young adult life. After many laughs and running up the clock, I had to let Boseman know the bad news. At the end of the month, I would no longer have the love line. I could hear the disappointment in his tone. He asked why. I explained that I had accepted a new position out of state. In all honesty, it was only two hours away, but who cared. Well, apparently, he did because he made me an offer I could not refuse.

"Well, I have two weeks to convince you to come have dinner with me."

A few days later, the blue light on my love line phone lit up and the phone rang. I typically didn't have the ringer on or the phone out unless it was work time. But something told me to answer it.

"Hello, is this Miss Delilah?"

"Yes, this is she."

"I'm Marion Champion. I was given your number by Mister Manning regarding an executive position we have available."

In my mind, I was like, *No he didn't.* This man didn't have access to my real name or resume. *Why would he think this is a good idea?*

"Miss Delilah, are you there?"

Clearing my throat, I answered, "Yes, I'm here. When would you like for me to come in for an interview?

"We have an opening available for Saturday at eleven a.m. Will that work for you?"

"Excuse me, are you typically open on Saturdays?" I wanted to get a clear understanding because I hated working on weekends.

"No, we aren't. However, because you come highly recommended by Mister Manning, we are willing to accommodate you."

"Well, yes, I will be there."

She then proceeded to give me the details of the job, pay, work, and travel schedule before hanging up.

About fifteen minutes later, my phone rang again. I knew exactly who it was—Boseman. "Hey, Delilah, my girl. I heard you have an interview Saturday."

"Why did you do that, Boseman?"

"I know I was wrong, but when you mentioned you were moving because of money, I figured I would call my connections and help you. I believe you are a great woman, Delilah ... under all those secrets."

"Boseman, you don't know my real name. You barely know who I am."

"Delilah, stop it. I know this may sound strange, but I don't care. I just want to get to know you. After the interview Saturday, we will talk."

I aborted my phone call and went straight into panic mode. *If I accept this job, this man will know my address, phone number, real name. That's too much. Think, Charlie.*

Just then, my pride and joy came into my room to talk. Phoenix warmed my heart. I could use an extra $50k a year to give her the world. She would be worth me making the adjustment. *It might not be too bad after all*, I thought.

That Saturday morning, I walked in that interview with so much confidence. I nailed every question. However, I immediately became intimidated by the many beautiful, smart black women that worked there. I had never seen so much poise, grace, and articulation in one room in my life. After the interview, they asked me to wait in the lobby. After about five minutes passed, a tall, handsome young man approached me. He first asked if I was waiting for someone. Then he asked if I would like to tour the building. I was very obliged.

As he took me on this tour, I was taken aback by the details of the building's structure, art, state-of-the-art technology, lavatory, employee café, gym, and so much more that the company had to offer. But what really got me was the relaxation room.

As we completed the tour, the tall, handsome, chocolate, edible young man explained that the building was owned by a black man. And, as part of the new-hire process, the owner would like to meet me.

"Like in right now?"

"Yes, like in right now," he said, smiling.

"Wait … am I hired?"

"I would like to say yes, you are."

My heart began to beat so fast. I was wondering why there were so many people at work on a Saturday, when the office was not typically open on Saturdays.

The young man interrupted my thoughts by asking me to follow him to meet the owner. We walked down a long hallway with beautiful pieces of art painted by both professionals and children. Then it dawned on me. Boseman! It was Boseman … he was the owner. He had created a way to meet me in person. Before approaching the door. I told the young man I needed to use the ladies' room. I made an excuse to go to the first floor to grab my purse.

Ha ha, Boseman! You will not meet me today. We will meet on my own terms and my timing, mister. I grabbed my things and slipped out the door. I walked as fast as I could to my car. Before I could unlock the car door, Boseman called.

"Why did you leave? Did you not want the job?"

"Boseman, we will not do this on your terms. You do not and will not dictate or force me into meeting you. I have a job. Do not play with me like that."

He apologized for overstepping his boundaries and trying to trick me into meeting him without regard for how I felt about it.

"Now that we got that straight, do you want the job?"

"No, I do not," I said, knowing good and well I didn't mean it. I needed and wanted that fifty thousand dollars.

"Why not, Delilah? Is it not paying you enough? I can have them increase the pay."

"Boseman, why are you so desperately trying to help me? You have a wife and kid you have to take care of."

"Didn't I tell you she left me? And besides, she is not my wife. We lived together for seven years. She slept with my best friend and had a baby by another man."

"I thought she was your daughter."

"No, I can't have kids. I told you that. I just was too ashamed of not being able to give her what she wanted, so I accepted the child as mine. I will take care of the child forever. Just because her mommy's trifling doesn't mean I have to be."

"I need you to pay for this childcare and the parking ticket today before the office closes."

"Oh, Delilah, that's nothing. I will do anything for you, Charlie … Oops, Delilah. How much do you need? I'll Zinc it to you."

"Okay Ian, please do."

A moment of silence passed. "Delilah, how do you know my name?" Boseman said, breaking the silence.

"Is it a problem, Ian Boseman Manning?"

"No, I just never go by Ian."

"I know your name the same way you know my name. Research, negro."

"I'm gonna Zinc the money to you now. You think about my offer," Boseman said, before hanging up without giving me the chance to respond.

A whole week had passed, and I hadn't heard anything regarding the job or Ian. However, just when I was picking my little princess up from school, my phone rang. The voice on the other end spoke. "Miss MacClemore, this is Toni with Avery Productile. I would like to inform you that your background has been cleared and we are now ready to move forward with the hiring process. That's if you're still interested in the position. Are you available to sign paperwork Tuesday at nine o'clock? The pay will be one hundred and twenty-five thousand, annually. Benefits also include after school care, child tutoring, transportation, and an hour and a half lunch break, and you'll be off every other Monday. How does that work for you?"

I was taken aback by the pay ... fifty-five thousand dollars more. I began to stammer over my words. All I could think of was how Phoenix and I could have a much better lifestyle. I could get rid of the love line and help my mom more.

"Thank you, Toni, for the offer, but I will have to decline the position."

She seemed shocked to hear my response.

"Well, Miss MacClemore, may I ask why?"

"Yes, you may ask why." We both listened to each other breath heavily through the phone for what seemed like an hour, although it was only a few seconds.

"Miss MacClemore, are you there?"

"Yes, I'm here."

"I will need a decline reason. You don't have to give detailed information, however. We just need a code in the file for HR training. Could you let us know why you are declining the position?"

"Sure, honestly, I do not think it would be something I'm genuinely interested in. I would rather work somewhere I am making a difference. Like making a difference in someone's life verses advancing someone's net worth. Have a great day, Toni." Sweat gushed out of every pore in my skin. *Why did I just do something that stupid?*

Whew chile, I felt like a ton of bricks hit me in the stomach. I can't believe my pride and ego let me pass up that annual income. But I was not going to sell my soul for Ian. He was not worth it. My new job was paying me ninety-thousand dollars annually, and I could still provide the same lifestyle for my kid and help my mom.

Baby girl and I decided to skip our normal schedule and go have dinner at the park. This time, we drove to the white folk park where it was nice and clean. I grabbed some Panny Bread sandwiches, chips, and juice from the sandwich shop. We sang our favorite prayer as we walked hand-in-hand looking for a spot to set up. We were giggling and joking with one another when I happened to look up and see a man running in our direction. He was close enough that I could tell he was good looking and sexy. I don't think he was paying attention, just focusing ahead while on his run.

I couldn't see his face with the shades and what appeared to be a whole oxygen mask over his mouth. *He must be athletic.*

Just as we finished setting up, Phoenix said she had to use the restroom. When I turned my back to pick up the basket, she ran off. I scanned the immediate area and zeroed in on her a few feet ahead. There she was … talking to the man who was running. I was furious, pissed, hot, angry and was determined to beat her little arse to pieces when I caught up to her. I ran up to her with every intention of reprimanding her, but my plan was hijacked when

I heard a familiar voice call my name. It was *his* voice. I couldn't turn around; I felt stuck. Why did I always feel paralyzed around attractive men? Geesh! *Is this who I think it is?*

"Hello, Charlie. How are you?"

"You know my mommy?"

My cheeks felt flushed. I was speechless. My jaws dropped. *Is this who I think it is?* This is what his body looks like? He runs like this every day? He looked like the Ken doll in human form. During one of our Love Line calls, he mentioned having a black father who was a Black Panther and a Hispanic mother who was an active member of the NAACP. But he never mentioned he was the most gorgeous man God created. The way the sun glistened off his skin, the silky hair, and his 6'7" athletic frame would make any woman melt. Not to forget to mention his sexy voice. It sounded better in person than over the telephone.

Fixing my hair and clearing my throat, I tried to pretend to not be in shock. I turned around and half-smiled.

"My mommy like you. She was looking at you earlier," Phoenix and her big mouth said, looking at Boseman and then at me and back and Boseman. I was so embarrassed.

"Sir, how do you know my mommy's name?" Phoenix asked, tugging at Boseman's shirt.

Before he had a chance to answer, I started speaking. "So ... um um ... Ian, it's been a while. How are you? How's the firm?"

"Everything is going well," he said, looking at me and then at Phoenix. I guess he was trying to see the resemblance between the two of us.

"By the way, this is my little busy nine-year-old."

"Hello, pretty girl," he replied, looking down at her. He paused for a minute and directed his attention toward me. "You know, I took your advice. I have a therapist that I am seeing now. I have cut off all extracurricular activity for now until I become whole with myself."

"That's very good," I told him. An awkward moment invaded our space as we stood, staring at each other.

"Are y'all gonna kiss or something because I want to play," Phoenix said, jumping up and down.

"She's a little firecracker like her mom, I see," Boseman spouted, chuckling.

"Yes, she is my whole world, and I love everything about her fire," I defended.

"What's your name, beautiful?" he asked my daughter.

"I'm not allowed to tell any stranger my name. My mom will beat my bottom and take my dollies. We have to practice privacy because people are bad," Phoenix recited, just as she had been directed by me.

"Do you think I'm bad and your mommy is talking to me?"

"Nope, but Mommy don't play about me, so I'm not saying!"

"Well, okay. If I take you and your mom out on a date, will you tell me your name then?"

"Are you a killer man or beater or a thief?" she questioned him.

Boseman bent down eye to eye with her. "No, baby girl. I am none of those things. I will protect you from people."

I must have pinched his neck so hard that he almost fell over.

"Mommy, can we go on a date with stranger-danger-running man? He won't hurt us," she asked, looking up at me.

Now, I was a little perturbed that he had gotten my daughter involved in the twist. "How about I take your number, Ian? We chat first then arrange a date for the three of us."

"Yay! Yay! Yay! We going on a date … we going on a date!" Baby girl must have sang that little song repeatedly at least a million times.

On the drive home, Phoenix fell asleep. I took the opportunity to call Ian. He picked up on the first ring. After hearing his song of apologies for the first few minutes and how he couldn't get me off his mind, I agreed to go out with him on a date. "Yes, I will go out with you. You have eight days to change my mind about you before I move on."

"Are you really moving?" he said.

"Yes. My life … oh, never mind. Yes, I'm moving."

"So that means … oh never mind. So, you declined the job?"

"Yes, I did. Did they not tell you?"

"I must've missed the message because I had no clue. I guess this means that I better start today. Can I bring you guys dinner?"

"No, not today."

"Can we meet for breakfast at seven tomorrow morning?"

"No!" I said.

"Nine?"

"Yes, Ian." I finally obliged.

"I'm so excited to see you, Charlie. I promise to make the next week worth your time. I want to wow you and your daughter too. You are going to want to marry me in five days, Charlie, and baby girl will have nothing to worry about, ever. I promise to love and take care of her more than your mind could imagine. I love you, Charlie."

What the fuck? If I hear another "I love you, Charlie" from a man that don't know me ...

We ended the call, and Phoenix and I went about the rest of our day.

While getting dressed the next morning, I received a text message from Ian. I figured I should start calling him Ian rather than Boseman. It seemed more personal and warm.

I'll have a car to pick you and baby girl up around eight thirty. Wear a nice sundress and bring shades. The driver will drop her at school and then bring you to me. Today will be full of surprises. If you could take off today, I will reimburse your earnings times three. Please, no declines.

I obliged without hesitation, texting back: *I accept.*

When I opened the door for the driver, I was surprised to see that it was the same guy who had given me a tour of the building during the interview.

"Hi, Miss MacClemore. Remember me?"

"Yes, I remember your face but not your name," I said as I stepped out of the house.

"I'm Mason. I'll be driving you today."

"Why thank you, Mason. May I ask where we're going?"

"I've been given specific instructions to not give you details. But what I do know is that it is a surprise that you're going to love."

"Oh, really?!"

"Get used to seeing me, Miss MacClemore. I think the boss really likes you. He has never allowed us into his personal life before."

As we pulled off, Mason complimented Phoenix, telling her how pretty she looked.

"Phoenix, say 'Thank you,'" I reminded her.

"Who is this man driving us, Mommy?"

"Phoenix, mind your manners. Say thank you."

Phoenix took it upon herself to pry for more information. "Excuse me, sir, but are you the man that was running in the park? Are you still taking me and Mommy on a date?"

Mason began to stutter. "No, I am not."

"Phoenix! Shhh … don't be rude," I said, hoping to stop the verbal bleed. Phoenix dropped her head, trying to hide her embarrassment. She hated being scolded in front of others. I tried not to do it, but sometimes, it was warranted, and this was one of those times.

We dropped Phoenix off at school and proceeded about our way. I must've been sleepier than I thought because I dozed off during the ride and was awakened by a tap on my shoulder.

"We're here," Mason whispered, passing me a warm towel to clean my face and handing me a breath mint.

"Where are we?" I said, admiring the place. The place was exactly what it looked like in magazines. I was in shock. "Oh, my goodness! This can't be!" I said. I was happy that I had worn one of my best sundresses and my matching rhinestone sandals.

Ian had remembered every detail of our conversation. "I'm at the summer home of one of the most famous couples on television," I said, admiring the grounds of the mansion.

"Yes, you are. The Smiths and Mr. Boseman are best friends. They have a wonderful afternoon planned for you," Mason said, as he popped open the trunk of the car. "Mr. Boseman has a bag with changing clothes in the trunk for you. He said he knew you wouldn't pack a bag."

Ian walked up, smiling from ear to ear. "There you are. Finally, you made it. Thank you, Mason, for taking care of her and the precious cargo. You're welcome to stay and enjoy the festivities. If you don't want to stay, we'll just see you at four o'clock."

The day was beautiful: lunch by the pool, outdoor massage, personal chef, live music, spoken word, lots of famous people. But to top it all off, Ian had hired my favorite musician, song writer and vocalist Usher, to sing to me. I couldn't believe it. He had outdone himself with this first date. *I think I'm in love. But only in love with the idea of love and things.*

During the drive home, Ian asked how I enjoyed our first date and asked if he could see me the next day for another date. After all, he only had five days to keep me here or I was bouncing. I could see Mason looking at me from the rearview mirror as if he was anxious to hear my response.

"What about work? My kid? Ian, I can't stop life to date you for two weeks."

"Charlie, you gave me a few days to make you change

your mind. Quit your job. I got you for the next two weeks. Baby girl will be taken care of. She can join us on some of our outings or I can see you during the day only. This weekend, we can take Phoenix wherever she wants to go. She did ask me to date you, didn't she? What better way to date her mom than to have her with us?"

"Boseman, why are you so adamant about dating me?"

"Charlie, I have known you for two years. I hear you when you talk. I listen with intent and understanding. I have never had any woman around my staff. Hell, my ex didn't meet my staff until my daughter was born. This means something. Trust me, Charlie."

I could feel myself panicking. I hadn't dated anyone serious since I divorced my daughter's father and got out of that foolish situation with Terrance. I exhaled before responding. "Let's allow it to happen naturally, Ian, if it's going to happen. I'm not ready to date seriously with a young daughter."

He understood but still insisted that he see me the next day. As we approached my daughter's school, he grabbed my hand and said it again. "I do want to love you for real, Charlie."

I hurriedly jumped out of the car to avoid saying anything back. I could see Phoenix running toward me with tears in her eyes. "Baby, what's wrong with you? Did someone hurt you?"

"Mommy, I think Daddy found us. He came to the school today. When I saw him, I hid behind the desk. The security didn't let him in. I was scared, Mommy! I thought he was going to take me again."

Ian jumped out of the car, noticing the obvious excited state Phoenix was in. "What's wrong? What happened to her?"

"It's a long story, Ian. I can't talk about it now. We have to leave. I think I'm going to take that job sooner than later. Take us home."

"Charlie, do I need to stay with you?"

"No … no… please, leave me the fuck alone, Ian. I don't love you. I like you. I don't want to hurt you. You deserve real love, Ian."

Once we arrived home, I found a note on my door: *I found you, bitch.*

Ian couldn't help but to see the note too. "Charlie, let me help you, whatever it is."

"Ian, please go in and search my place for me, please."

He did as I requested but didn't find anyone in the house. "No one is in here," he yelled out to me.

I grabbed clothes for Phoenix and me, enough that could last us for about a week. "Baby girl, we're going to stay with Mr. Boseman, okay? Get all the toys you want to take with you," I said to Phoenix as I escorted her to her room.

I was in total survival mode. I really didn't have time to think, just to act. I needed to find the time to pack my place up. Staying with Ian was only a temporary arrangement; I needed that apartment to be ready sooner.

After getting semi-situated at Ian's house, a lavish six-thousand-square-foot home, Ian and I decided to sit on the veranda to enjoy the evening breeze. I'd put Phoenix to bed around eight. She had an exhausting day, having gone through the traumatic experience of her father's attempted kidnapping once before, my baby girl needed comfort. Mason handed us a glass of red wine before heading back into the house. As I sat back and thought about it, Mason was around more than I thought he should have been. In addition to paying me a plethora of compliments whenever we were alone, I often noticed how he'd stare at me all the time, even when I was with Ian. I decided to get some questions answered.

"Does Mason live with you, Ian?"

"No, sweetheart. He lives down the street in one of my rental properties."

"Does he pay rent?"

"Yes, I pay him for the jobs he performs. In return, he pays his rent, just like any regular tenant. He has to be a man and provide for himself. I just met the young man about three years ago. He was adamant about working for me. He moved here from New York and was looking for a fresh start. After his mom moved back south to take care of her elderly mother, he decided to come this way." He provided more in-depth responses than I thought he would, so I took it upon myself to dig a little deeper.

"Have you ever met his mom?" I asked.

"Actually, no I haven't. I have spoken to her briefly on

the phone a few times. His mom was strange to me. She would always decline my Facetime calls but then call right back. Whenever I would chat with her, she would keep the conversation very brief."

"Well, Ian, what do you know about him? He seems to not really have a personal life, almost like he's here with you sunup to sundown.

"Well, Charlie, that's none of my business. He was hired to do a job, and I pay him well to do it. Let's shower and get to bed, honey. We have long day ahead of us," Ian suggested.

I woke up the next morning to breakfast in bed, with Ian and baby girl, who was fully dressed, both standing beside the bed watching me. I didn't want to panic. I was praying that Ian hadn't helped my daughter get dressed. So, I politely asked, "Who got you dressed, sweetness?"

"The cleaning lady."

"Did she help you with your morning wash up?"

"Yep. She stood outside the door and told me to do this that … and do this … and do that. Now hurry, I have a big surprise for you."

"Honey, you have school. You have to go to school."

"No, I don't. Mr. Boseman brought school to me today, and he said I don't have to go."

Clenching my teeth, I looked up at Ian. He got the picture. Looking down at Phoenix, he said, "Honey, can you step out for a moment? I would like to speak to your mom alone.

I didn't wait for him to explain; I went right in on him. "Ian, you cannot make decisions like this regarding my child without consulting me. She's not your daughter."

"I know … I know, Charlie. But I believe your ex-husband was at her school this morning."

"I don't know what's going on, but I figured I was helping."

"How do you know that, Ian?"

"I called the school to inform them Phoenix would be late, and that's when the receptionist then informed me that there was a man at the school claiming to be Phoenix's father and demanding to see her."

"Okay, that takes care of that earlier. What about when she has to go to school later?"

"Girl, get out the bed and get dressed. We are going to take care of this idiot who keeps following you."

"No, no," I said as I began to sob. "He will try to kill us. He is crazy." I told Ian the whole truth about why I was running. In my state of vulnerability, I shared with Ian that the reason Phoenix and I moved was because of the fraud case, my entanglement with Terrance, and because my ex-husband was crazy. "Ian, hear me when I say this, George is no person to play with. He will kill us and not feel an ounce of guilt."

At this point, I could barely utter my words. My cry

intensified. I know Ian could feel the heart of my emotional pain. As I wept, he held me so tight.

"I will protect you, Charlie. You have to trust me. Can you let me handle it?"

"Of course, I will. Just keep me and my baby protected."

I knew a man with money meant power. I was willing to relinquish my power for him to protect us.

The weekend was so relaxing. Baby girl reminded me that they had a big surprise for me every day. Finally, the day came. Ian asked me to wear white.

"We are going to an all-white event and taking baby girl with us." Without argument, I obliged his request. The house staff was smiling from ear to ear all day, whispering so I wouldn't get wind of any of the day's plans.

When I walked into Ian's closet, I noticed that not one trace of his ex was there. All her things were truly gone. Not one thing of hers was in the house.

"Ian, may I ask you something?" I said from the walk-in closet.

"Yes, but let's hurry to avoid being late."

"What happened to all of her things?"

With a deep sigh, he responded. "Charlie, why, baby? She has moved on and so have I."

"Ian, tell me."

"Tell you what, Charlie?"

"Details?"

"Today? Now? We have serious business to take care of," Ian said, snatching a shirt off a hanger.

"Yes. Today. Now," I said, looking directly at him.

"Well, after she moved out, she had planned to come back to pick everything up. I boxed our daughter's things and mailed them. I donated my ex's things to Goodwill," he said with a smirk on his face.

I rolled my eyes, shook my head, and walked into the bathroom to finish getting dressed. As I sat at the vanity, I thought about how Ian hadn't tried to have sex with me at all, which made me wonder, *What if his middleman doesn't work?*

My thoughts were interrupted by the sound of a bell and the voice of my daughter. "Mommy, come on. We are going to leave you."

"Okay, I'm coming," I said as I exited the room with a beautiful white fitted dress on with a split up to the thigh, showing off my sun-kissed skin. The back was cut low. I finally let my natural hair down, wore light make up and a beautiful white smile to match.

The entire crew looked so shocked when they saw me. Mason's eyes almost popped out of his head. They had never seen me in anything so form fitting. Everyone was caught off guard.

"We had no idea you had all of that under those baggy, sexy clothes you wear," Mr. Perkins announced with a loud laugh. Mr. Perkins was Ian's right-hand man. Every decision Ian made had to be approved by Mr. Perkins.

"Mommy, are you ready for surprise number one?"

"Yes, baby, I am."

"Close your eyes. Grab my hand and walk this way." I followed Phoenix through what seemed like a large matrix.

"Open your eyes!" Phoenix said with excitement.

When I opened my eyes, I saw the most beautiful room I had ever seen. "Ian," I said. Your daughter's room is gorgeous." I felt like I had stepped into a magazine.

"Do you want to tell her or me, baby girl?" Ian said to Phoenix.

"Mommy, it's *my* room. We have been working on it for two days. We fooled you, Mommy."

As I walked in closer, I noticed the artwork, our pictures, new chairs, new bed, a vanity, a walk-in closet, a playroom, and a popcorn station. Shit, the whole world was in the room.

"Ian, I got dressed up for this? I can't play with her in this dress. Besides, we don't live here. You've done a lot for visitors."

"Mommy, we do ... oops, never mind," my daughter said. "Okay, your turn Mr. Booosssman!" Phoenix said, looking at Ian.

"Charlie, I love you, and I want the world to know. Com'on, let's go eat."

"Let me grab my purse."

"You don't need it."

We walked outside by the pool. Beautiful white tulips covered the pool. Beautiful candles lit the walkway as soft music played in the background. "Are we not going to the car?"

"Yes, Charlie. It's this way."

"Where is my baby?" I said, turning to look for Phoenix.

"Don't worry, Mason has her. Just give me five minutes," Ian said.

As we walked around the pool, I noticed a part of the house I had never seen before. In this area, there were fancy tables and chairs. A live band stood on a makeshift stage as they played my favorite songs. Then suddenly, white balloons began to float to the sky.

Where is my daughter?" I asked again.

"She is right over there with the staff."

As I looked around, my mom, brothers, sisters, cousins, friends, and aunts were all standing behind me. I began to weep as I ran to greet them.

"Mom, I've missed you so much."

As we were all hugging and crying and kissing, Phoenix appeared with a mic in her hand.

"Mommy! Mommy! Where are you? Come here for the big surprise!"

As I made my way over to her. She read her poem to me. "Roses are red; Violets are blue. Sugar is sweet; Now turn around …"

When I turned around, Ian was on bended knees. "Will you marry me?" he asked.

Baby girl jumped up and down. "I told you I could keep a secret! Say yes, Mommy. Say yes!"

I looked at my family. They were all nodding. I reluctantly said, "Yes, crazy man." We all danced the night away. Ian and I had the most passionate kiss ever that night. Ian was so gentle with me.

By the next morning, Ian had the whole wedding planned. "We will be married in three days, Charlie."

"How? We don't have a marriage license," I said.

"Charlie, I can get whatever I want when I want it. We pick up the license tomorrow at noon."

While sitting at the table next to my mom, I stared at her and admired her love and prayers for me. It took her awhile to become the woman she now was. The woman she used to be was a woman that was likened to hell on wheels.

I couldn't stop hugging and kissing her. I didn't realize how much I missed my mother. She was truly the center of my joy, although God had proved to me to be my lifeline. In her older years, my mother reminded me of my granny. My granny was a praying woman. I knew it was her prayers that helped me get as far as I had gotten.

I reached over and whispered to my mom, "Do you think I should marry him?"

She replied, "Only when you stop sleeping with his son, brother, or whoever that driver man is. This man claims he loves you. You cannot sleep with the help, Charlie."

My eyes must have popped out of their sockets. "Mom, how do you know that?"

"I know you, Charlie. Any fool can see you guys are messing around. Ian … he knows it too. He's just waiting for the right time to tell you. Be careful with Ian. He's going to try to control you. Make sure you keep the upper hand. I told him all this fancy shit don't impress me; he needs to get right with God first. Now, that's impressive. You know your brothers and sisters loving all this free shit. He gave all of them five thousand dollars each to come out here for their inconvenience. Chile, please; that's chump change to my girl. Charlie, I hope you have a plan this time."

Having walked up on us, Ian interrupted before I could respond. "I hope you were having a positive conversation about me, mother-in-law."

"It was half positive, Ian. I just told my daughter to not trust you fully. You're nice but sneaky. Anything else you wanna know?" my mother said unapologetically.

"Okay, what's next on the agenda today?" I said to Ian.

"Let's go find you a dress," he insisted.

Once we arrived at the bridal salon, a beautiful young lady greeted me with a glass of champagne and a danish.

"Miss soon-to-be Manning, we have pre-selected you twenty gowns to choose from. Your mother and future husband came in yesterday to pick them out for you, just to make the process easier on you. If you would like more to choose from, I would love to help you. You have a four-hour reservation," a representative from the bridal boutique said.

I tried on dress after dress after dress. I didn't like any of them. I wanted something simple but elegant. After all, we were getting married in our backyard. I didn't have that many friends that I truly trusted, and both of my sisters were expecting, so it was just gonna be me and Phoenix walking down the aisle.

The day finally came. It was a quick four days to prepare and pull off a whole wedding. I was told to just show up. And that's exactly what I did. I was proud of the decision. I trusted my mom's exquisite decorum and Ian's priceless taste.

The staffer walked in to let me know I had less than two hours before the wedding. I hadn't seen Ian all day. My mother came in to remind us of all the trouble they had to pay for me to get out of trouble the last time a man had proposed to me.

"Mom, I was totally innocent. You know that. Terrance's sideline hoe set me up. I'm glad that heifer's in jail. She deserved those fifteen years," I snapped back.

"Charlie, I really liked Terrance. He didn't have an agenda, this Ian negro does. You better be careful."

"Mom, you and Daddy taught me how to lie, cheat, steal, and manipulate well. I got this. I love you, Mom, with all my heart, and you know I'll do everything for you and my precious baby girl. Trust me? Okay?"

"It's time, Mrs. Manning."

Our song came on: "Alone Together" by Daley.

Just as my dad grabbed my hand to walk me down the aisle, Ian asked the musician to stop the music.

I heard a tap on the mic. "Everyone, thank you for joining us today. I regretfully inform you that there will be no wedding. I just learned that I have a son, Mason, who didn't tell me he was my son. And he has been working with me and sleeping with my fiancée for the last five weeks. I guess that's why you couldn't sleep with me," Ian said, turning to look at me. "So, enjoy the food and take your gifts back. Charlie, you and your family need to get out of my house."

I blurted out in loud laughter and tapped the opposite mic. "My friends and family, you are very welcome to stay. They aren't leaving our house. Ian, we are already married. No pre-nup was signed. Half of everything is mine. So, you can leave, Ian. We are about to enjoy the party."

Ian was furious. He had lost control. The idiot wasn't aware it was my private investigator who mailed him the pictures of Mason and me and revealed Mason's true identity.

"Ian, the next time you have a PI follow me, make sure you don't hire *my* PI." I laughed and walked back into the "not wedding," party. "We rich, bitch," I said out loud as I pranced past Ian.

CHAPTER 7

*L*ies I told, I almost believed them myself.

Before having my daughter, I would pretend I was a famous pole dancer. That was the highest I thought of myself because my self-esteem was so low. I felt like my mom suffered from bipolar disorder. The highs and lows in her personality scared me. When my mom would become upset, she called me stupid every chance she got. The things I thought wouldn't cause her to become angry would make her react in an absurd manner. But the things that I felt might have bothered her didn't; she held her cool. It was difficult trying not to tick her off. She blamed it on menopause. I guess she experienced menopause the first twenty-one years of my life. I didn't recognize how it bothered me to be called an idiot, stupid, or dumb. But one thing's for sure, her and my father taught me how to be a pimp with no apologies.

When I was about sixteen years old, I had to tell my parents the worst news that, apparently, a daughter could tell her parents—I was pregnant. But not only was I pregnant … I was pregnant with twins. I waited to tell them because I didn't want my boyfriend or parents to convince me to have an abortion. I thought my mother would hate me forever. It was my very first time having sex. I can recall that day like it was yesterday. I remember all the pain, both physically and emotionally. Needless to say, I lost the babies two weeks after sharing the bad news with my parents. I believed that is the reason why I hated having sex, believe it or not. I could use one good partner that I didn't have to attach to emotionally and be good the rest of my life.

On my way to the hospital, my mom informed me that I was having a miscarriage. She was crying harder than I was. The pain was unbearable. All I could do was scream. There were no tears, just yells and screams. I think my tear ducts stop working.

"Charlie, my angel, you have to calm down now, sweetness. Mommy's right here. Breathe, baby. We're almost there."

"Where is my daddy, Mommy? I want my daddy. Please stop the pain." I could feel her hurt from my request of my father. He was very supportive of me during my pregnancy. My dad didn't treat me like my mom did; she was so mean and hateful. On the other hand, I probably deserved it. My brothers had more respect for her than I did. They feared her, but I did not.

"I called your daddy, Charlie. He will meet us there."

As we arrived at the ER, my daddy was there yelling at the receptionist, requesting to see me. But the receptionist was so calm in explaining that I was not there. Just as he was about to cuss her out again, my mom called his name.

"Charles, shut up that noise. She is right here."

My daddy picked me up, put me in a wheelchair, and demanded the staff save the babies. My daddy loved kids, and I don't know why. He was rarely home. He didn't know what to do with us. He just gave us what we wanted. But he always told us he loved us, all day every day.

"Daddy, why do you smell like perfume?" My senses were acute, being pregnant; I could smell the corn in the cornfield ten miles away.

My dad pinched me so hard and whispered, "Shut up, Char!" Guess he didn't want my mother to know that he had been with one of his slutty women. I know my mother knew he was cheating, but you have to be a bold somebody to come around your wife smelling like another woman. The only reason I believe it happened this time was because it was an emergency; he didn't have time to wash and change his clothes.

As the nurse pushed me to the back, blood flowed down my legs like a river.

Dr. Nixon had the most pleasant bedside manner. "Miss Charlie, it is clear that you've had a spontaneous abortion. We will have to perform a D&C. I'm so sorry sweety."

The doctor went out to inform my family that they could not save the babies. I had a D&C and would be discharged in a few hours. My daddy came in the room with his "assistant," which was code for the new lady he was sleeping with.

"Where is my mommy?"

"She left to pick up your brothers from practice, Char. She will be back."

"Miss Cindy, why are you here?"

"When your dad told me about what happened, I had to come check on you."

"Oh, yeah?" I said. "Daddy, you and Cindy need to leave now. You both smell like her perfume and sex. When mom comes back, there will be hell to pay."

Cindy had a baffled look on her face. "Yes, Cindy, I know about you and my father. Get in line with the rest of these hoes. Don't steal from him, don't call him at home, and don't disrespect my mother. She is aware and will have no problem with kicking your ass in the hospital room if she feels like it."

"Char, watch your mouth!" my father barked.

I must have looked at him like I was gonna beat him into next week.

"Okay, Char. Daddy's sorry. It's your mom; she—"

I stopped him. "Don't blame my mom for your infidelity. You have cheated on her my whole life. Cindy, I'm sixteen. I have seen at least sixteen women my dad has been with in the last twelve years. Run while you can."

"Charles, why are you having this conversation with a child?" Cindy said, shocked that I was confronting my dad about his raggedness.

"Although my dad is a horrible husband, he is a great father. I consider him my superhero, my best friend, my everything. He is teaching me to not choose a man like him. You're the dummy here, Cindy."

Just when my daddy was about to say something crazy, the hospital phone rang.

"Hello, Charlie. Is your daddy there with you?" my mother said.

"Yes, ma'am." I answered.

"Put him on the phone."

"Daddy, mom would like to talk to you," I said, handing him the phone.

I heard him say, "Yes, baby, I will. Okay … love you." The call ended.

"Char, Daddy gotta run errands for Mom. She should be here in ten minutes."

"Bye, Cindy," I said sarcastically. "Daddy, come back, okay."

"Daddy will be back to pick you and your mommy up when you're being discharged in two hours, baby girl. Daddy loves you."

My mom arrived not five minutes after my daddy left. I could hear mom whispering on the phone with some man. She thought I was asleep. "Mom, who are you talking to?"

"Oh, this Kurt, baby." Kurt was my gay uncle. She was not talking to my uncle Kurt. I was his favorite niece. If he knew I was in the hospital, he would've been at the hospital. So, I pretended to go back to sleep.

I was struggling to hear what exactly my mom was saying to this man on the other end of the phone. Then my baby daddy walked in, ruining the whole mood.

"Hey, Miss MacClemore. Is she okay? Why didn't you all call me?"

My mom replied, "Your lil' punk arse the reason she in here. You just had to take her virginity and get her pregnant at the same dayum time."

"Mom, please stop! It's not just his fault. I am just as responsible for what happened."

By this time, the nurse came in, explaining I would be released in the next few hours. Then my favorite man walked in just in time.

"Hey, Daddy!"

"Hey, baby girl. How are you?" No matter what, my dad always treated my mom like a queen in my presence. He leaned over and kissed my mom's forehead, gave her a hug, and then passed her a bouquet of flowers for being an amazing wife.

As my dad turned his back, my mom rolled her eyes. I admired my mom for staying with my dad for almost twenty years. I was their only daughter and oldest of the three children. I was curious as to why my mom stayed with my dad when I was a little girl. I saw her cry, heard the constant fights, witnessed the different women my dad had personal relationships with, and saw how my brothers accepted the false narrative that women were not to be respected but used as a lay partner.

During the drive home, I decided to share with my mom that she didn't have to stay with Dad for us. We understood that her happiness was more important than being committed to misery. And I also told her I knew she had been seeing Mister Sir. My mom didn't blink an eye. As she turned on our street, she simply said, "The 'he' you're assuming I'm seeing is a 'she.' But what I do and who I'm seeing is none of your business."

My mouth fell open. "You're cheating on my daddy with a woman?" I blurted out.

There was dead silence. I almost jumped out of the window of the moving car. She was really exploring sexually. I guessed that love was love and sex was sex. I didn't judge my mom. I understood. She needed love with no boundaries and emotional connection. I earned a new-found respect for my mom. She trusted me with sharing her most intimate secret and respected my maturity.

"Charlie, did I shock you?"

"Well ... yes, Mom. I wasn't expecting that."

"Are you going to leave my daddy?"

"No. I will never divorce your dad. I love him too much, and I know God committed me to him. I'm just battling with his years of infidelity. Charlie, he teaches you that men use women. I see you turning into him and your brothers as well. I've never known how to be transparent with kids, but I just know I don't want you to allow men to misuse your mind, heart, or body, Charlie. I earnestly pray for you, Charlie. You need a mind change and a spiritual shift, as your granny would say. I know I haven't shown up for you like you may desire, but this experience today has taught me more about what I need to do as a mom than what you need as a child. I love you, Charlie. Mommy's sorry I wasn't there for you. But I leave you with this, Charlie—Do not let a man use you. Get them before they get you!"

Those words resonated in my mind for the rest of my life. I handled relationships as such … *I'll get you before you get me.*

CHAPTER 8

ack to Ian, Mason, and me. The party was everything one could imagine. All my friends didn't
blink an eye at Ian's findings. They all knew me
so well. Younger men were easier for me to manipulate,
and, of course, younger men had way more sexual energy.
Hell, I guessed everyone knew that I was sleeping with
Mason. He posted subliminal messages on his InstaBook
page every day. I think it's what tipped Ian off. To be
completely honest, Mason and I hit it off instantly when
he gave me the tour of Avery Productiles. He asked for
my number; not only that, but he called me five minutes
later. We talked on the phone seemingly all evening. That
night after my daughter fell asleep, he came over. When I
tell you it was the best sex I had ever had!

The first time we had sex was so funny. Mason wore
an elephant costume to bed. He wouldn't take it off. He
wanted me to ride him like an elephant, he'd said. That's

exactly what I did. I rode his face and his dick until he got tired.

Although he was a few years younger than me, he made me feel like a twenty-one-year-old again, sexually and emotionally.

Mason was fully aware Ian and I were not sleeping together. One, I told him, and two, I was with Ian by day and Mason by night after my daughter would fall asleep. Phoenix even walked in the room one night, complaining of a belly ache. I was so thankful it was dark in my room. She had no idea Mason was in the bed. I pulled her in the bed on my side as I kicked Mason to move over.

"Mommy, what's that smell?"

"What does it smell like, baby?" I asked.

"It smells like smoke and a weird smell."

I smirked to myself. I originally thought she was referring to the smell of Mason's wild cologne. I rubbed her belly until she fell into a deep slumber. Her being able to smell his strong cologne was the cue for Mason to leave. This child could smell the bidis smoke and our sex all in one. I knew opening a window wouldn't get rid of the smell.

As we were all dancing at the party, my mom pulled me to the side. "Charlie where is your husband and boyfriend/stepson?"

"Mom, I don't know. Nor do I care."

"Well, you should, Char, because while you're having

a party with your friends, you need to pay attention to what's going on."

"Mom, I am married to a millionaire. I don't care what's going on. I broke it off with Mason last week. I'll explain later."

Just as we were talking, Ian came over and grabbed my hand and pulled me in the direction of our bedroom. I snatched my hand from him. "What are you doing? Don't ever grab me like that."

"Girl, get your ass in this room." He began to kiss me passionately. Between each kiss, he said, "Charlie, I have waited for this moment. I love and hate you right now, but I'm ready to consummate this marriage." He was so aggressive and sensual all in one. It turned me on in some strange way. I was mesmerized by this monstrous behavior and aggression.

All I could think was that the sex better be good. He was panting and breathing hard, snatching off my clothes. He picked me up and took me in the bathroom. My eyes began to water. There were dozens upon dozens of red and pink rose pedals all over the room. Candles were lit and soft jazz played in the background. "Ian, this is beautiful, but we have guests, baby," I said.

"No, Charlie, you have guests. But since you refuse to not be my wife, we are at least going to do what husbands and wives do."

Not even twenty seconds later, he dumped me in the bathtub, wetting my hair, my face, and soaking my panties. My makeup was runny, my lashes were hanging on by a thread, and my panties were now sagging on me. "What are you doing, Ian?" I said as he jumped in with his pants on.

"I'm doing me, Charlie."

The next thing I knew, a camera crew entered.

"What are they doing here? What are you doing, Ian?"

"Fellas, Delilah, the Love Line queen, married me and is trying to take all of my money," he yelled. "After sleeping with my son, Delilah, if this is what you want, this is what you're going to get."

I guess he thought he would get a reaction out of me, but I played right along with him.

"Yep, I'm Delilah, and all he said is true. We are now going to see if his penis can work as hard as his mouth is moving right now."

Ian had a bewildered look. "I hate you so much, but I love you more than I hate you."

"Shut up and make love to me, old fool," I said, pulling him close to me.

The cameras stopped, but the music continued to play. It was exactly what I expected it to be. Ian made love to me like I have never experienced, love or sex, even better than his son, Mason. He was very passionate, soft, gentle, and warm. He kissed every part of my body. I felt our souls collide as we became one.

What seemed like forever was only a forty-five-minute session of lovemaking. We quickly showered. I allowed my natural curls to hang. Ian suggested I wear the pajamas he bought me. He said he would wear the matching set he had.

"Ian, why did you hire a camera crew? What was your purpose of that?"

"Honestly, Char, I really wanted to piss you off and hurt you like I felt. After I saw it wasn't working, I decided to go with Plan B."

"What's Plan B?"

"You will see," Ian said.

As we walked out of the room, he asked me to close my eyes. He escorted me to the elevator down to the basement. "Don't look, Charlie."

I could hear Phoenix snickering.

"Open your eyes."

"Surprise!" Everyone had on their pajamas. There were pictures of us everywhere. Everybody who was somebody from Hollywood was there.

"All of this for me?" I said, shocked.

"Yes, Charlie. It's your wedding weekend. We will make the best of it," Ian said.

The DJ began to play my favorite jam. Just as we were about to toast, Mr. Baldwin asked the guests to step outside for the fireworks show. It was so beautiful. Just as we turned to walk in, Ian yelled, "Gift number eight!" In came a beautiful tan Rolls Royce. I fell to my knees. *It is no way this man can love me like this. I'm so undeserving.*

I thought I would use him and keep going. He was truly forgiving … that quickly.

My dad came over and looked in my eyes. "Charlie, baby girl. You are my angel. But this man seems off to Daddy. Please be careful. We will be gone in two days, and I just don't trust him and all this fancy stuff. If you want Daddy to help you, I will. However, you need to have a real plan, an evacuation plan. Where is Mason? He was at the wedding, but then disappeared. And now it seems like Ian has disappeared too. Please be careful, Charlie," my daddy said.

"May I have my wife for a moment, father-in-law?"

My daddy smiled big. "Yes, son-in-law;" with the fake, "I'm so happy for you two."

CHAPTER 9

My so-called wedding-turned-party was the best weekend I'd had in a long time. Saying see you later to my parents and siblings was the hard part. I hadn't seen them in so long. I hated to see them go back to the good state of Mississippi.

I tried calling Mason nearly fifty times, but I got no answer. So, I decided to ask Ian what happened to him. The mention of Mason's name made Ian's blood boil. "Charlie, do not ever ask me about him again."

"Ian, you act as though he planned to hurt you. He and I started seeing each other before I considered becoming serious with you. When you asked me to marry you, he respected you, and we never saw each other again. He is your son, Ian. You have to step up to the plate to be a father to him."

"How do you know that, Charlie?"

"The same way you know, Ian Boseman Manning. He never asked you for anything. He did as he was told. He had so much admiration for you, Ian. You have to give it a chance. Did you contact his mother?" I asked.

"No. His mother and I dated so long ago, I barely remember her."

"His mom is dying, Ian. Mason takes care of her. If you have done something bad to him, please let me know."

Moments later, I received another call from his mother. I looked down at my cellphone, watching it ring until it stopped and transferred over to the voicemail system. I took a deep breath and turned to Ian. "His mom has called my phone a million times looking for her son. What did you do to him?"

"Dayum, Charlie. I, I, I …"

"Did you kill him, Ian?" Ian didn't answer. "Oh my God, Ian!"

"No, I just roughed him up a little bit … a few broken ribs, broken leg, arm, busted nose. He's in the hospital. He will be fine," Ian said without flinching.

"Which hospital, Ian? You better tell me right now."

"Or what, Charlie? What in the hell are you going to do?"

"Ian, don't doubt me. I'm from the 'hood … the 'hood, hood, nigga. I will eat you up and spit you out without thinking twice if you try me."

We both pulled our guns on each other simultaneously. I welcomed the gun show. Just as I was about to speak, Phoenix came into the room. We both hid our guns.

"Mommy, I'm hungry."

"Can you ask Maria or Ella in the kitchen to make you breakfast?"

"No, I don't know what they're saying, and I don't speak Chinese."

Ian interrupted. "It's Spanish, Phoenix, not Chinese. You are almost ten years old, so it's time for you to learn a different language, don't you think, Daddy's big girl?"

"You are not my daddy. You are my bonus pops. But yes, I agree with you."

Putting the guns away, we both walked away from each other.

Later that morning, I must have called every hospital in the city. I had to think outside of the box. I finally found Mason a whole three hours away at Guiding Light Hospital. I asked the head chambermaid, Marie, to watch after Phoenix, and I took a three-hour trip to Guiding Light Hospital to check on Mason.

Standing at the nurses' station, I said, "Excuse me, excuse me, ma'am."

"How may I help you?" one of the nurses replied in an agitated tone.

As I began explaining to the nurse who I was there to see, Mason appeared from around the corner, being pushed in a wheelchair. I attempted to control my reaction, but my maladroit facial expression said it all.

"Judging by your facial expression, I look that bad, huh?" Mason questioned.

"Can you give the nurse permission to add my name to your visitation list?" I asked.

Mason nodded. That was about all he could do, physically.

Back in his hospital room, it seemed like it took forever for the nurse assistant to review Mason's medical chart. I understood it was proper protocol to discuss her therapy plans. My anxiousness was getting the best of me.

"Ma'am, can you please leave us alone for a moment. I'm sure those same instructions will be in the discharge papers," I said with a hint of agitation in my voice.

The nurse's assistant slammed the medical chart into the holder at the bottom of his hospital bed and rolled her eyes at me as she left the room.

"Mason, I am so sorry this happened. Why didn't you call me? What happened to you? Who did this? How did you get here?" I had a million questions running through my head.

"Charlie, don't ask me questions you know the answer to."

I got an opportunity to speak with his doctor, who said Mason would be fine, but he needed to stay in the hospital for another week or so. He also mentioned that Mason would need to go to physical therapy for four to six weeks after being released from the hospital. I promised Mason I would be there with him every step of the way.

Every day, I would turn my location off on my phone, catch the train to the Lancaster Station Two bus stop, and walk the remainder of the way to the hospital. I created a loving relationship with the hospital staff because I needed them to trust me with his aftercare.

Although Ian and I had a blissful relationship, I knew I wasn't in love with him, and he knew it also. Every moment I spent with Mason, I saw more of his beautiful soul. Although he was nine years younger than me, he was the best thing I had ever known. We laughed, talked, and decided to be totally naked with each other, mentally. He shared with me his childhood dreams, why his mom didn't tell him about his father, and that he had a five-year-old son he named Avery, after his dad's business.

I learned that Mason's only desire was to build a relationship with his biological father, then tell him that he was his son. Mason was Ian's clone. Although Mason and I hadn't had sex in forever, our chemistry was still amazing. All I could think of was how so disrespectful it was of me to be married to his father but totally in love with him.

When it was nearing the time for Mason to be discharged, I had to pick Phoenix up from school and have dinner cooked before Ian made it home. At the same time, I had to make transportation arrangements for Mason to make his way home. That was the hard part, talking Ian into allowing him to continue to stay at his property. After

I explained to Ian that I was Mason's only emergency contact he had stored in his phone, he was okay with me helping Mason in this manner. I lied, but I needed to get Ian's buy-in. And when that seemed like it might not be enough, I resorted to a sermon.

"Ian, if you have compassion, any compassion for *all* mankind, including Mason, no matter what he's done … He's still your flesh and blood. I know it might be hard for you, but you have to forgive him for what he's done. Just ask God to help you do the right thing. You can't turn your back on your own son."

"Charlie, don't you think it's funny that you slept with both me and my son?"

"No, Ian, I don't. Do you want to face the hard truth about this whole situation? We are all guilty, and that includes you too. Until you're able to face your truth as well, sir, you'll only see everyone else's wrong and not your own."

"Charlie, I felt betrayed by both of you."

"Ian, you are the master of betrayal."

"I tell you what, Charlie. He can stay as long as he can pay rent. If he can't, then he gotta go."

"Ian, you know he is not working. I don't know how much money he's saved."

"Charlie, why can't he go back with his mom?"

"Why can't you help your son? Why can't you help your son that you don't know? Why can't you ever be responsible for your faults, Ian?"

"Charlie, Mighty, Mymy, Delilah … whoever the hell you are today. He is a grown-ass man. If he can't pay, he can't stay. You got that?! Now get out of my face with this bull."

Little did Ian know, I wired Mason seventy-five thousand dollars to his account to cover all his bills for twelve months.

Of course, I was running late to meet the therapist at Mason's place at four thirty. This was the first time I had to explain to a ten-year-old to not tell Mommy's business. With baby girl Phoenix in tow, I met Mason and his therapist, Jane, at the front door. I had a cleaning company come in to clean his space, rearrange the furniture, and install handicapped equipment in the restroom.

"Hey, Phoenix. What's up, big girl?" Mason said when he saw Phoenix. She raced over to hug Mason as tight as she could.

"Mr. Mas, I really missed you. What happened to you? Why is it a secret?"

Mason had limited mobility in his legs, and he hated help. Although he had the wheelchair to assist him, until he regained all his strength, he refused help from anyone. I guessed that was his manhood and pride speaking.

As he rolled himself through the house, he noticed his furniture was rearranged, things were missing, and the bathroom was handicap equipped. I thought I was doing something to help him. He was not pleased.

"Get this shit out of my bathroom. Move my furniture

back where I had it, Charlie. I am not handicapped. I do not need nor want your help."

Phoenix began to cry. "Why are you talking to my mommy like that?" Mason immediately apologized and began to weep himself. I could see the sorrow in his eyes. He grabbed and hugged both Phoenix and me so tight.

"I love you both so much. I thank you for being here for me, Charlie, because I have no one. I didn't mean what I said to your mommy, Phoenix. Please forgive me."

We all sat in the silence, crying for what felt like love. Moments later, Phoenix asked if she could play with the neighbor's kids in the backyard. Mason and I sat out back to watch them play. Mason grabbed my hand and looked me in the eye.

"Charlie, I love you more than I should. I literally wake up every day thinking of you. The thought of losing you broke my heart. It is because of you I am still here today. I need you to know that, Charlie, and I know you love me too. I know you only married my dad to run away from your past."

As I began to speak, Mason placed his finger over my lips. "Shhhh … there is more, Charlie. You asked why he did this to me. I never answered you. I need you to know the truth."

"Mason, I have to get home. Ian will be there soon," I said, attempting to get up.

"Charlie, call me as soon as you can in the morning.

This is urgent. I have hired guards to watch my home and you. You gotta trust me."

Entering our beautiful estate, something told me to pack a bag for the two of us. I hid our personal paperwork, jewelry, and any item I could make money from by selling or bringing to the pawnshop in that bag. I took the items to one of my close friend's homes and hid it in her attic without her knowing. Very anxious to know what Mason had to tell me, I had the driver take me to TJ's and Inky's Coffee Shop.

I made small talk with the owners of the shop, planned a play date with TJ, and off I went, purposely leaving my phone at the shop. It was a place I knew would be safe and a place where Ian would expect me to be, as he traced my whereabouts.

I caught a cab to Mason's place. I changed my clothes and put on a wig, just in case Ian's nosy friends were watching. Mason was sitting, waiting for me. "Charlie, you're late. Where have you been?"

"I had to run an errand this morning."

"What did you do, lose your phone? I called your Google number several times."

"I must have left it at the coffee shop," I said.

I made him breakfast and lunch. "Mason, what is it you want to talk to me about?"

"Charlie, I never told you why Ian had his men try to kill me. I found out some information that I shouldn't have known. It is about you and your daughter's father.

111

Once Ian figured out that I knew, it was too late for him to annul the marriage, but he didn't want you to know what was going on. He figured I would tell because he knew all along we were sleeping together. He just didn't know you would fall for me."

"Damn it, Mason, what is it?" I was anxious to know.

"Ian and your ex are planning to kill you, Charlie. Your ex, Terrance, is actually Ian's best friend from college. They have known each other all their lives. Ian keeps the company afloat with your ex's drug money."

"What? He sells drugs?" I said, totally mystified. I had no knowledge.

"Yes, that's why Terrance wanted you so bad, to get back at your ex."

"What?" I said as I grabbed my chest.

"You know your friend Ralph?

"Yeah," I said.

"Well, Terrance hired him to be your doctor. You knew Ralph was married to a man, but Terrance paid off his student loans, his parents' home, and told him he would kill him if he didn't go along with it. Ralph is actually a licensed vocational nurse. He's not a doctor. They knew you didn't know any of us. Your ex, George, has been a part of the street life all of his life."

"George's lame ass sold drugs? I knew he was a drug user. Never would have thought he would sell drugs."

"Yes, and you are the only woman he has ever loved. He has been looking for you for years. He knew money and stability would lock you in with Ian. They have been planning this for years. The bad part about it is, Ian actually fell in love with you too. Charlie, I need you to get you and Phoenix out of here. Don't go back to that house. No one is there to protect you."

I was steaming hot but trembling with both tears and fear. "What was your plan, Mason, huh? How were you planning to hurt me?"

"Charlie, I love you I would never—"

I abruptly interrupted his "I love you" spill. "Shut up your lies. I know about the many women you slept with during our short run. You think I'm stupid too, huh? You came over to my place smelling like them. You don't think I know about your addiction to sex and porn. Let me count the women you have paid for sex since we are no longer together, Mason. Miss Tate, yeah that was the girl you used to get your rocks off when I wasn't available. Oh, let's not forget Destiny, the long-term married one you slept with. Oh, let's not forget to mention Sharonda, Nikki, Tiffaney, Toni, Candace, and should I go on? You literally had scheduled weekly dates with all of them. I had to find out the hard way by the STD you gave me. But, stupid me. You went without seeing them for a whole two weeks, and I thought the love was real. Your dumb ass laid up in a hospital bed. Not one of them came to your rescue? You couldn't remember anyone's number?"

This was probably not the opportune time to allow my emotions to lead my thinking, but I had to let Mason know that I knew what he had been doing and I didn't trust him either.

"Charlie, calm down. It was you who said for me to do me, that you wouldn't have a relationship with me. It was you who said do me. It was you, Charlie, who refused to love me in return. I would have stopped all of that. I love sex, I do, but I would rather make love to you every day and every night."

"Of course, you would, negro. Your bitch ass can't walk and need assistance."

I walked into his room to grab the gun I hid under his bed.

"Charlie, wait. What are you doing? Please don't kill me."

"Stupid ass ... you're not worth the bullets. You are the payoff. Happy Father's Day. We are five weeks pregnant." This gun is for your protection. You should keep it close to you in case ..." I paused.

"In case what, Charlie?"

Before I could answer, Mason's eyes filled with tears. "Are you serious? Are you having my baby, Charlie?"

"*My* baby, Mason. You're going to pay for him or her." I stormed out to the door.

On my way to the coffee shop, a million thoughts flooded my mind. Oh, how I hated Ian. How could I have allowed someone to trample over my heart. How did I miss Ian's red flags? Being Delilah led me, yet again, to run. I cried, "God, I am tired of running."

I knew he would be waiting for me, so I had to put my game face on. I had to stay two steps ahead of Ian. I devised a plan to leave.

As I approached the coffee shop, of course, you can guess who was there. Ian! "Where have you been, Charlie? TJ told me you left about twenty minutes ago but that you forgot your phone." I guess TJ knew Ian was crazy, because she lied for me. I had been gone for about three hours.

"Yeah, I realized I didn't have it. I came back to get it."

"Oh, sweetie, I have called you fifty times. I was worried."

I kissed the devil's forehead. "I'm perfectly fine. Where are you headed, Ian?" I asked.

"I have to meet a client in Duluth at two o'clock. I was wondering if you were up for the ride with me. We could go shopping, have dinner, and maybe a little fun."

"Nope. Thanks for asking. I do not want to go have fun. I promised Phoenix a play date today."

I rushed home and packed as much as I could. If I didn't take this opportunity to leave, I would be a dead woman by the next day. I gave the entire staff the evening off with pay. I had my PI come over and help me with security cameras. I had twenty-four hours to do everything I needed to do. I had my mom fly in, and I put her up in a nice hotel with Phoenix. I explained to her I was going away for a little while. I gave her the codes to the cards. I gave her my car to trade in for an SUV in her name. I wired her two-hundred thousand to last her for at least three years to take care of my daughter.

"Honey, please tell me what's going on," my mother begged.

"Mom, no, you cannot be a part of this. You and Daddy are set right now. I put everything in Phoenix's name just in case he tries to take the house from you. Just pay for my baby's schooling." I broke down in tears. "Why did you do this to me, Mom? Why did you create this monster in me? I don't want to be her anymore. I'm tired of running!" I screamed.

My mom held me so tight and didn't let go for what felt like eternity.

"Mommy, Ian and George are plotting to kill me. You know I'm not going to let that happen."

"Char, did you call the police? Do your brothers know? Oh, my goodness, Charlie what are you going to do? I can't just let them hurt you. I'm calling your daddy."

I knocked the phone out of my mom's hand. "If you call anyone from this phone today, you are going to get me killed. Just trust me."

When I arrived back at home, the moving company was there cleaning out the house. I told them to not wrap anything, to just put it on the truck. Just as the truck was leaving the property. I could see Ian coming in from the roadway.

He'd called eight times in four minutes. I hid downstairs in the basement and called him back.

"Hey, baby. I have some company coming over to-night. Where are you?" Ian said as soon as he picked up.

"I'm on my way home," I lied.

"Oh good. The company's with me. Can't wait to see the surprised look on your face."

I watched Ian get out of the car. I saw him talking to someone, but I couldn't make out who it was. The other person stood at the car, and Ian walked down the walkway and into the house. I could hear him in a yelling match with himself. "I'm going to kill this, bitch," he said.

I chuckled. Then my phone rang. "Charlie, where are you?" Ian yelled.

Just then, a text from Mason popped up on my phone. I didn't bother to read it. I just typed back: *Shut the fuck up, Mason.* Then, I hit the "Block This Person," option. I peered out of the window again. This time, I got a better look at the person standing outside of the car. It was George!

I eased my way upstairs and peered through the side crack of the basement door. I had to get them both in the same room. Then, the doorbell rang. *Shit, who in the fuck at the door now?* I wondered.

"Hello, Mrs. MacClemore. You're just the lady I want to see," Ian said, pulling my mother into the living room.

Mom? What the hell is she doing here, I wondered.

Ian grabbed my mom by her throat. "Where in the fuck is your daughter?" George walked in from the kitchen. "You see, Miss Mac, you thought it would be me who would beat your ass," he said as he lit a cigarette.

My mom shook her head and began to cry.

I took a deep breath before bursting through the basement door.

"Here I am, Ian! It's me that you want. Let my mom go!"

As he let my mom go, George pulled a gun. Before he could shoot, I shot him in the face. Simultaneously, my mom pulled her thirty-eight caliber and shot Ian in the stomach.

"I got this and proof he tried to kill me. Leave now!" But my mother refused to leave. She was the only witness I had to explain everything to the police.

"No man will ever hurt you again," she said as she stood over Ian's slumped body and put another bullet in him. This time, in his head.

At some point, I completely blanked out. I don't remember much of what happened. I saw my life flash in front of me. Protecting my mom was my only thought, and I recalled pulling the trigger as I looked at George, his face reminding me of all the ugly things he'd done to both me and Phoenix in the past.

"Mommy, you gotta get out of here. The cops will be here soon. I can't have you at the scene of the crime." I had so many thoughts going through my head. I had never shot anyone before. Well, in honesty, I had ... just had never killed anyone before. There I was, carrying another man's baby, married to a dead man, who was in cahoots with my ex-husband.

We devised a plan to make sure our stories matched. We couldn't afford for either of us to go to jail for murder. It had to be self-defense.

CHAPTER 10

It was Saturday and another all-day visit from my mom, Mason, and Phoenix. Every week, she would ask when I'd be coming home. The crazy part was that I wasn't charged with murder for Ian or George's deaths. They got me on fraud. George, my now dead ex-husband, had somehow created accounts in my name and was moving money. Money laundering. That's what they call it.

They gave me a five-year sentence. I would get out on good behavior in three.

In prison, I found out why I became Delilah on the love line. I recalled the many stories of the Bible my grandmother would read to me. As I grew up, I never wanted to be associated as a harlot, although in some form or fashion, that's what I became. I read the good book while I was in prison. I knew I was in search of something or someone to identify myself with and blame. I found out who. There she was, in the good book, telling all my business.

In the biblical story, a weak man falls in love with Delilah and then the Philistines use her to learn the secret of his strength. Delilah and Samson were apparently lovers but were never married. Sounded a lot like me. I had many lovers and had no intention of marrying; my only intention was just to use and abuse them.

Delilah was treacherous. She accepted a bribe to reveal Samson's strength. You see, money can buy anything, even your so-called integrity, if you let it. According to what the text said, the man loved Delilah. She never loved him and had no qualms about betraying him.

My grandmother told me that story in the Bible repeatedly. She must have seen something in the spiritual realm and wanted to help me from becoming a dreaded harlot. That's what they called them back then. Today, we call them other names, like hoe and slut. But in all my granny's efforts to sway me differently, none of them worked, apparently. I played right into the devil's hand.

Sitting in the yard, gazing up at the sky, I could have sworn the sun winked at me. Prison had saved me. I saw a part of myself that I had never seen. I learned that the prison was always in my mind first. Each day gave me an opportunity to learn how to love myself. I had life growing in my womb when I first started serving my sentence. I refused for my babies to experience the same hostile environment Phoenix experienced. Right then, it clicked—God had to enter my heart and be accepted as my personal savior. That was the true message my granny's prayers were about. I had gotten to a place where I couldn't lean, run, or turn to anyone but Jesus.

I lived the lying, deceptive life of Delilah for many years. It was time for me to take that weapon of destruction off. If becoming Delilah meant I had to sit here for three to five years to become whole, then it was worth it. I refused to give up on me. After all, as the saying goes, life is what you make it.

Dear Sis,

If you see yourself in any of these characters, please submit to God. He truly is the only way. No sin is new under the sun.

Blessings,
Charlie "Delilah" MacClemore

DISCUSSION QUESTIONS

1. Who was your favorite character and why?

2. What part of the book do you most relate to you?

3. Do you know a Charlie or are you a Charlie?

4. Do you think Charlie's parents realized how much their relationship shaped Charlie?

5. Do you want a sequel?

6. How much of Charlie's behavior do you think will rub off on Phoenix?

7. If you could tell Charlie anything, what would you tell her?

8. Did you instantly feel sorry for Ralph?

9. Why do you think George was attached to Charlie?

10. What part of the book pissed you off the most? Why?